The Courageous Quest of Little Leo

Virtue Series

Callum West

Published by Kids Publishing, 2024.

This is a work of fiction. Similarities to real people, places, or events are entirely coincidental.

THE COURAGEOUS QUEST OF LITTLE LEO

First edition. November 19, 2024.

Copyright © 2024 Callum West.

ISBN: 979-8230634782

Written by Callum West.

Table of Contents

Preface 1
Chapter 1: The Shy Lion Cub 2
Chapter 2: Penny's Plight 6
Chapter 3: The Legend of the Singing Tree 11
Chapter 4: Setting Out on the Journey 15
Chapter 5: Meeting Grizelda the Gorilla 20
Chapter 6: The Wisdom of Ula the Owl 24
Chapter 7: The Raging River and the Crocodile Guard 28
Chapter 8: The Challenge of the Thistle Grove 31
Chapter 9: Sariah the Snake's Clever Test 34
Chapter 10: Encounters with the Mischievous Monkeys 38
Chapter 11: Facing the Foggy Forest 42
Chapter 12: The Wise Words of Balthazar the Bear 46
Chapter 13: Braving the Night in the Jungle 50
Chapter 14: The Enchanted Clearing 55
Chapter 15: The Return Journey 59
Chapter 16: The Celebration of Song 64
Chapter 17: The Gift of Gratitude 68
Chapter 18: The New Path Forward 72
Chapter 19: The Great Jungle Council 76
Chapter 20: The Unexpected Visitor 80
Chapter 21: The Storm's Trial 84
Chapter 22: A Gift from the Stars 88
Chapter 23: The Teaching Tree 92
Chapter 24: The Journey of a New Friend 96
Chapter 25: The Legacy of Courage 100

Preface

The idea for *The Courageous Quest of Little Leo* began as a simple story of a young lion on an adventure, but it quickly grew into a tale of courage, unity, and friendship.

This book is for those who believe that bravery is more than facing challenges alone—it's about opening our hearts, supporting one another, and finding strength in connection. Each character, from the wise owl to the gentle elephant, embodies qualities we all cherish: patience, kindness, and resilience.

Through Linden's journey, I hope readers will see that true courage isn't found in isolation but in the bonds we form and the lessons we share. May this story inspire young readers and remind us all that no matter where life takes us, courage is found in the heart and is strengthened by the love we give and receive.

Chapter 1: The Shy Lion Cub

In the heart of the vast and vibrant jungle, a young lion cub named Linden lived with his family. Linden was not your typical lion cub; while many young lions pranced proudly around, Linden often found himself quietly observing from a distance. The jungle was a magnificent place, buzzing with life and color, but it was also vast and sometimes overwhelming. Linden loved his family and his friends dearly, but he often felt a nervous flutter in his chest, a small feeling that whispered, "What if something goes wrong?"

Linden's timid nature was something of a mystery in the animal kingdom, especially among the lions. Lions were renowned for their bravery and boldness. His father, Roark, was the strongest and most courageous lion of them all, often leading the pride with a mighty roar that echoed through the jungle. Linden admired his father greatly, but he sometimes felt like he could never live up to that powerful roar or fearless heart. While other lion cubs would practice pouncing and roaring, Linden preferred to listen to stories from the older animals or watch the fireflies dance at dusk.

Despite his shy nature, Linden had a few very close friends, and none were closer to him than Penny, a colorful and lively parrot. Penny loved to chat and sing, often filling the jungle air with her cheerful tunes. The two friends couldn't have been more different, yet they were inseparable. While Penny chirped away with excitement, Linden would listen, offering a quiet but steady presence that Penny deeply appreciated. Penny's songs were loved by all, and her voice was a gift she treasured, sharing it freely with everyone in the jungle.

One sunny morning, while Linden was lying under the shade of a large baobab tree, Penny flew down beside him, her feathers ruffled and her eyes wide with worry. Linden immediately sensed something was wrong. Penny tried to chirp a greeting, but no sound came out. She opened her beak again, struggling to make a sound, but only a faint whisper emerged. Her voice was gone.

"Penny! What happened?" Linden asked, his soft eyes widening with concern.

"I don't know, Linden!" Penny mouthed silently, unable to speak. Her eyes filled with fear as she realized just how serious her situation was. For a parrot like Penny, her voice wasn't just a way to communicate; it was a vital part of who she was. Without her voice, how would she warn her family of danger? How would she sing her songs to bring joy to others?

Linden felt a pang in his heart as he watched his friend struggle. He wanted to help, but he wasn't sure how. Linden's heart was gentle and compassionate, but courage wasn't something he often relied upon. Just the thought of facing something unknown made his paws feel shaky. But as he looked at Penny's sad, silent eyes, he felt something stir within him. He wanted to help, and maybe, just maybe, he could find a way.

Later that day, Linden overheard a conversation between an elderly tortoise named Tovo and some young animals. Tovo was known for his ancient wisdom and stories that seemed older than the jungle itself. Tovo spoke slowly and thoughtfully, his voice rich with experience.

"Many years ago," Tovo began, "there was a magical singing tree hidden deep within the jungle. Its leaves held a special power. They say that anyone who lost their voice could regain it by plucking a leaf from the tree and holding it close. But," Tovo paused, his eyes glinting with mystery, "the journey to find the tree is long and dangerous. Only those who are truly brave ever make it there."

Linden's ears perked up, and his heart began to beat faster. Could this be the answer to Penny's problem? But as he listened, a familiar voice inside him whispered, "But what if something goes wrong? What if you're not brave enough?" He tried to shake the thought away, but it clung to him like a shadow.

That night, Linden lay in his den, unable to sleep. The idea of finding the singing tree haunted his mind. Penny needed help, and while he was scared, the thought of leaving her alone with her silent fear felt worse. He imagined her sitting quietly in her tree, unable to sing, feeling helpless. Something inside him seemed to grow, urging him to act. He knew he wasn't brave, but maybe he could find a way to be, just this once.

The next morning, Linden approached his mother, Liora. She was gentle but strong, a lioness who had always believed in the power of kindness and quiet strength.

"Mother," Linden began, his voice shaking slightly, "I think I want to find the singing tree. Penny has lost her voice, and I think... I think I might be able to help her."

Liora looked at her son, her eyes softening with understanding. She knew how much courage it took for Linden to even think about such a journey. "My dear Linden," she said gently, "sometimes courage doesn't feel like a roar. Sometimes it's as quiet as a whisper, and yet it moves mountains. If you feel this is the right thing to do, then perhaps you're braver than you realize."

Her words filled Linden with a strange mix of fear and determination. Maybe he didn't need to roar like his father to be courageous. Maybe, just maybe, he could find his own way of being brave.

With a final hug from his mother and a quiet farewell, Linden set off early the next morning. The jungle was filled with the sounds of birds and insects, and the sunlight filtered through the trees in gentle rays. Linden walked slowly, his heart pounding, but each step seemed to give him a little more confidence.

As he ventured further into the jungle, the familiar sounds and sights of home began to fade, replaced by strange plants and unfamiliar noises. The jungle felt different here—wilder, more mysterious. Every now and then, Linden would glance back, tempted to turn around and return to the safety of his den. But thoughts of Penny and her silent struggle pushed him forward.

After hours of walking, Linden came to a small clearing where he saw a few animals gathered around a wise old owl named Ula. Ula was respected across the jungle for her wisdom, and she often shared advice with young animals trying to find their way.

"Ah, young lion," Ula said as she noticed Linden, "you seem to carry a heavy heart and a touch of fear. What brings you so far from home?"

Linden hesitated but found the courage to speak up. "My friend, Penny, has lost her voice. I heard about a singing tree that might help her, and... well, I want to find it for her."

Ula nodded thoughtfully. "Courage isn't the absence of fear, young one," she said, her eyes twinkling. "It's the choice to act despite it. Remember, every brave creature in this jungle has felt fear, but they found strength in their hearts to move forward. Keep going, and trust in yourself."

Her words lingered in Linden's mind as he left the clearing. As he continued his journey, he began to realize that maybe courage was something that could grow, something he could nurture with each step he took. He still felt scared, but a small, budding belief was beginning to take root within him.

With each step, Linden began to understand that courage was not a sudden leap but a series of small choices—a path of bravery, step by step. And with every step he took, Linden grew a little closer to becoming the lion he was meant to be.

Chapter 2: Penny's Plight

As Linden took each careful step through the dense jungle, thoughts of his friend Penny filled his mind. The colorful parrot had always been a light in the jungle, her voice echoing cheerfully through the trees as she sang songs that lifted everyone's spirits. She sang to welcome the morning sun, to celebrate the rain, and even to soothe the jungle animals at night. To Linden, Penny's voice was not just a song—it was a constant reminder of joy, kindness, and courage.

Now, that cherished voice was gone.

Linden recalled the fear in Penny's eyes as she tried to speak, her beak moving but no sound emerging. For a creature who lived by her voice, this silence was not just troubling; it was terrifying. Penny's voice was more than just a song for her family. She used it to warn her loved ones of predators, to call her young ones back home, and to share important messages across the jungle. Without her voice, Penny felt powerless, and the entire jungle felt a little emptier.

Linden's heart ached for his friend, but as he continued his journey, a new feeling grew within him—a strange mix of determination and fear. He still wasn't sure he could find the courage to face all that lay ahead, yet he knew he couldn't turn back. This wasn't just about finding the singing tree; it was about helping someone he deeply cared for, even if it meant facing things he feared.

The jungle grew denser as Linden moved forward, and the morning light began to dim under the thick canopy. Linden took a deep breath, steeling himself. As he walked, every shadow and sound seemed magnified, and his mind raced with "what if" scenarios. What if he got lost? What if he encountered a dangerous animal? What if he failed to find the singing tree at all? The doubts clawed at him, but he thought of Penny and took another step.

A soft rustling sound interrupted his thoughts, and Linden stopped abruptly. His heart pounded as he scanned the surroundings, his eyes straining to make out any movement. Slowly, from behind a cluster of ferns, a young gazelle named Mavi appeared. Her large, gentle eyes sparkled with curiosity as she noticed Linden.

"Linden? What are you doing here, so far from home?" Mavi asked, her voice soft but surprised.

Linden took a deep breath, steadying himself. "I'm looking for the singing tree. Penny... she's lost her voice, and I want to help her get it back."

Mavi's eyes widened with understanding. "Oh, Linden! That's so brave of you. The singing tree is far away, and I've heard it's not easy to reach. There are many challenges along the way, and it's said only the truly courageous can find it."

Linden's stomach twisted at her words, but he nodded. "I know. I'm scared, but I have to try. Penny needs me."

Mavi smiled softly. "Courage isn't about not feeling fear, Linden. It's about doing something even when you're afraid. I believe you'll find a way."

Her words, gentle and sincere, brought a small spark of hope to Linden's heart. Maybe he could be brave, even if he was afraid. He thanked Mavi and continued on his path, the sound of her encouraging words lingering in his mind like a warm glow.

The jungle grew wilder and more mysterious as Linden ventured further. The trees stood taller, their branches stretching overhead like giant arms that blocked out most of the sunlight. Shadows crept along the ground, and unfamiliar calls echoed through the air. Linden gulped, feeling small and vulnerable, but he kept moving forward.

As he pushed through a tangle of vines, Linden suddenly found himself face-to-face with a towering banyan tree. Its roots twisted and coiled around the ground, creating a maze-like structure that was both beautiful and intimidating. Linden paused, uncertain. He had never seen a tree like this before, and the paths created by the roots seemed to stretch endlessly in every direction.

"Lost, are we?" a raspy voice called out, startling Linden. He looked around, trying to find the source of the voice.

To his surprise, a small, grizzled chameleon with shimmering scales appeared on one of the roots in front of him. The chameleon eyed Linden with an amused expression, his skin shifting colors with every tiny movement.

"Yes," Linden admitted, feeling slightly embarrassed. "I'm trying to find the singing tree. Do you know the way?"

The chameleon chuckled, his eyes twinkling mischievously. "Ah, the singing tree! Many have sought it, but few have found it. The path is not a simple one, young cub. It requires... let's say, a certain bravery." The chameleon paused, studying Linden thoughtfully. "Are you brave enough to face the trials that lie ahead?"

Linden hesitated. "I'm not sure," he replied honestly. "I'm scared. But my friend Penny needs her voice, and I can't let her down."

The chameleon nodded approvingly. "Bravery isn't measured by the absence of fear but by the strength to move forward despite it. Remember that, little cub." With that, the chameleon pointed with his tail toward a narrow, winding path between the roots. "Take this path, and you'll find the river. Beyond that lies the way to the singing tree."

Linden thanked the chameleon, his heart feeling a mixture of fear and resolve. With each new encounter, he learned a little more about courage. Maybe bravery wasn't something you had to feel all at once. Maybe it was something that grew, step by step, with each challenge faced.

The path the chameleon had directed him toward was narrow and winding, lined with thick roots that seemed to form a twisting maze. Linden carefully made his way forward, his small paws padding softly against the forest floor. The journey felt strange and endless, but he kept going, determined to help his friend.

Finally, after what felt like hours, Linden heard the sound of rushing water. His heart skipped a beat as he realized he had reached the river the chameleon had mentioned. But as he approached, his hope was replaced by anxiety. The river was wide and powerful, its waters churning and splashing against rocks. There was no easy way across, and the sight of the surging water made Linden's legs feel weak.

He took a deep breath, scanning the area, hoping to find a bridge or a shallow part he could cross. Instead, his eyes fell upon a large, shadowy figure resting by the riverbank. Linden's heart froze. It was Crooktail, the crocodile.

Crooktail was known throughout the jungle as a fierce and cunning guardian of the river. His rough, scaly skin and sharp teeth had scared many animals away, and he was not known for his kindness. Linden felt his courage falter as he stared at the powerful creature before him.

But just as Linden was about to back away, Crooktail's eyes snapped open, fixing on him with a curious, piercing gaze.

"Well, well," Crooktail rumbled, his voice deep and gravelly. "What brings a young lion cub to my river?"

Linden swallowed hard, gathering his thoughts. "I'm... I'm looking for the singing tree," he stammered, his voice barely more than a whisper. "My friend lost her voice, and I want to help her get it back."

Crooktail tilted his head, a hint of interest gleaming in his eyes. "The singing tree, you say? That's no small feat. And you, a young cub, think you're brave enough to find it?"

Linden felt a surge of determination rise within him. He didn't know if he was brave enough, but he couldn't give up now. "I... I'm afraid," he admitted, his voice trembling. "But my friend needs me, and I can't let her down."

Crooktail studied him in silence for a moment, his expression unreadable. Then, to Linden's surprise, the great crocodile nodded. "Fear is a companion of the brave, young one. Only those who understand fear can truly be courageous. If you are willing to cross, I will allow it—but be warned, the journey beyond is no less challenging."

With a final, encouraging look, Crooktail shifted to the side, allowing Linden a safe path to the riverbank. Linden nodded gratefully, his heart pounding as he carefully stepped forward. The churning river still looked terrifying, but Crooktail's words stayed with him, filling him with a newfound sense of strength. He took a deep breath and stepped onto the rocks, carefully making his way across with the guardian crocodile's watchful gaze following him.

Chapter 3: The Legend of the Singing Tree

Linden's heart was still racing as he crossed the river, each splash of water and slippery rock testing his balance and nerve. The jungle on the other side was quieter, more mysterious, as though it held secrets it shared with only the brave and curious. As he shook the water from his paws, Linden felt a small but growing pride. He'd crossed the river—a place he'd always been warned was dangerous, with its strong current and intimidating crocodile guardian. Yet, he had faced his fear and kept going.

But he knew this was just the beginning. The journey to the singing tree was far from over, and the jungle stretched endlessly before him. Every rustle of leaves or snap of a twig reminded him that he was far from the comforts of home. But Linden kept walking, his mind set on Penny and her silent beak. The thought of restoring her voice filled him with a resolve he hadn't felt before.

As he ventured deeper into the jungle, the sun began to set, casting long shadows that danced across the trees. Just as Linden started to wonder where he would sleep, he spotted a strange rock formation in the distance. The rocks seemed to glow with an otherworldly light, and nestled between them was a cave entrance. Hesitantly, Linden approached, hoping to find shelter for the night.

Inside the cave, he was met by an unexpected sight—a collection of animals sitting around a small, glowing fire, its light bouncing off the cave walls. The animals turned to look at him, and Linden recognized a familiar face among them: Tovo, the wise old tortoise.

"Linden!" Tovo greeted him warmly. "What brings you so far from home?"

Linden felt his cheeks warm with embarrassment but found his voice. "I'm looking for the singing tree," he said, surprised by the steadiness in his own voice. "My friend Penny... she's lost her voice, and I want to help her get it back."

Tovo's eyes sparkled with understanding, and he motioned for Linden to sit beside him. "Ah, the singing tree," Tovo murmured, his voice full of reverence. "You have embarked on a noble quest, young cub. Few seek the tree, and fewer still find it."

The other animals around the fire leaned in closer, curious about Linden's story. Linden glanced around, noticing an old hare, a wise owl, and even a gentle porcupine who seemed enthralled by Tovo's words.

"Why is the singing tree so hard to find?" Linden asked, his voice filled with both fear and excitement. He had heard the tree could restore voices, but he didn't fully understand why it was hidden so deeply.

Tovo closed his eyes, recalling the stories passed down through generations. "The singing tree is an ancient wonder of the jungle," he began. "It is said to be older than any of us can imagine, planted long ago by the jungle's first inhabitants. Its roots reach deep into the earth, drawing life from the heart of the jungle itself. The tree's leaves are filled with magic, capable of restoring not only voices but also courage, strength, and hope to those who need it most."

Linden's eyes widened. He hadn't realized the singing tree held such power. This wasn't just about finding a cure for Penny's voice—this was about tapping into something profoundly mysterious, a source of strength and healing that seemed to belong to the heart of the jungle itself.

"But," Tovo continued, his voice softening, "the tree does not give its gifts freely. It requires those who seek it to prove themselves, to show courage, kindness, and selflessness. Many have tried to find it, but few have had the heart to complete the journey."

Linden swallowed hard. He wasn't sure he had what it took to prove himself to such a powerful force. Yet the thought of Penny, her beak silently moving without sound, pushed him forward. He could feel his resolve deepening, even as he listened to Tovo's words.

"Would you tell me more about the journey?" Linden asked, his voice trembling but determined.

Tovo looked at him thoughtfully before speaking. "To reach the singing tree, you must pass through many trials. Some are tests of bravery, others of wisdom and kindness. You will meet creatures who may seem frightening, but who might offer you help if you show respect and compassion. And there are places you must enter alone, where only your courage will guide you."

Linden shivered, imagining the dangers he might face, but he nodded. "I'll do whatever it takes," he said softly, feeling the truth of his words. "I need to help my friend."

The other animals around the fire nodded approvingly, murmuring amongst themselves. The owl, her feathers shimmering in the firelight, spoke up. "If you are willing to face such challenges, then you have already begun to prove yourself," she said, her voice gentle but wise. "Courage is not always about feeling brave. Often, it's about feeling scared but still choosing to do what is right."

The animals around the fire shared stories of their own encounters with bravery, moments where they had to overcome fears to help others. The hare told a tale of standing up to a snake to protect her young ones, while the porcupine spoke of the time he had guided a group of lost animals through a storm. Each story filled Linden with a sense of hope, showing him that bravery came in many forms.

As the night wore on, Linden felt a sense of calm settle over him. Despite his fear, he realized he was not alone in his journey. Many others had faced challenges and fears, yet each had found courage within themselves when it was needed most. He felt a warmth growing inside him—a small ember of courage that he hoped would burn brighter with each passing day.

Eventually, the fire dimmed, and the animals began to drift off to sleep. Tovo placed a reassuring paw on Linden's shoulder. "Rest now, young one," he said softly. "Tomorrow brings a new part of your journey. Remember, courage grows with every step you take, even the small ones."

Linden curled up near the warmth of the dying fire, his mind filled with Tovo's words and the stories of the animals around him. The jungle seemed less intimidating now, its mysteries a little less daunting. He had learned that courage wasn't about being fearless but about moving forward, even when fear lingered in the shadows. And as he drifted off to sleep, he felt a quiet determination settle within him.

When morning arrived, the first rays of sunlight filtered through the cave's entrance, painting the stone walls with soft shades of orange and gold. Linden stretched, feeling surprisingly refreshed. As he stepped outside, he noticed Tovo waiting by the cave entrance, his wise eyes filled with kindness.

"Are you ready, Linden?" Tovo asked.

Linden took a deep breath, his heart steady. "Yes," he replied, his voice firm. "I'm ready."

With a nod, Tovo handed him a small bundle of herbs. "These will guide you to the next part of your journey," he said. "Hold them close, and you will find the strength you seek."

Chapter 4: Setting Out on the Journey

The sun was barely rising as Linden padded along a narrow path through the jungle, the morning light casting soft rays that danced across the forest floor. His heart thumped in his chest, partly with excitement and partly with fear, as he took one cautious step after another. The herbs Tovo had given him were tucked securely in a small pouch made of leaves, hanging from his neck like a little satchel. The calming scent reminded him of the warmth and encouragement he had received the night before, filling him with a renewed sense of purpose.

The path before him seemed endless, winding through tall grasses and over roots that twisted like ancient sculptures. Every now and then, Linden heard the distant calls of birds and the rustling of leaves in the breeze. It was peaceful but also strangely ominous. The jungle was vast and mysterious, holding secrets he had never dared to explore until now.

Linden's mind wandered to his friend Penny, imagining her sitting alone, trying in vain to chirp her songs. He missed the sound of her voice, the cheerful way she sang about the sunrise, the rain, and the simple joy of being alive. Penny's voice wasn't just any song—it was the song of the jungle itself. Her silence felt like a shadow over the world, and Linden felt a deep ache to bring back the joy she had always shared with everyone.

Lost in his thoughts, Linden didn't notice the rustling behind him until a soft voice called out, "Are you Linden?"

Linden spun around, startled, and saw a small, delicate creature with wings as clear as glass—a dragonfly with vibrant emerald and sapphire colors shimmering in the early light. Her name was Saphina, and she was known in the jungle as a wise and gentle creature who often helped guide lost travelers.

"Yes, I'm Linden," he replied, his voice soft but steady.

Saphina nodded, her wings fluttering gracefully. "Tovo told me about your journey to the singing tree," she said. "He sent me to guide you through the first part of the path. The way can be tricky, and there are places where the paths split. It's easy to get lost if you don't know where to go."

Linden's heart lifted with relief. "Thank you, Saphina. I would be grateful for your help."

With a gentle nod, Saphina flitted ahead of him, hovering just above the ground as she guided him through a maze of tall grasses and twisted vines. As they walked, Saphina shared small stories about the jungle, pointing out plants with strange colors and talking about the animals who used them for food or medicine.

"You know, bravery isn't always about fighting or facing something frightening," Saphina said as they walked. "Sometimes, bravery is about moving forward even when you don't know what lies ahead. It's trusting in yourself, even if you feel uncertain."

Linden listened, her words comforting him in ways he hadn't expected. He was learning that bravery wasn't some grand feeling he had to have all the time. It was a choice, a decision to keep moving forward because he cared for his friend.

After a while, they reached a wide clearing with a giant, twisted tree in the center. Its branches stretched out like arms reaching toward the sky, and at its base was a small, sparkling pool. The water was so clear that Linden could see his reflection perfectly, and he noticed the nervous flicker in his own eyes. It was strange to look at himself so closely, to see the small lion cub who had once been afraid of even venturing beyond his family's den.

"This is Reflection Pool," Saphina explained. "It's said that anyone who looks into its waters will see their true self—their fears, their hopes, and everything that makes them who they are. It's a place of self-discovery, and many who are on a journey stop here to understand themselves a little better."

Linden looked into the pool, feeling a strange pull as he gazed at his own reflection. For a moment, he saw himself as he was—a small, timid cub with a heart full of worries. But as he continued to stare, he began to see something else. There, in his reflection, was a determination he hadn't noticed before. Despite the fear in his eyes, there was also a spark, a glimmer of hope and courage that seemed to grow as he looked deeper.

"What do you see?" Saphina asked gently, her eyes filled with kindness.

Linden took a deep breath, trying to put his feelings into words. "I see... I see that I'm scared," he admitted, his voice soft. "But I also see that I care deeply about my friend, and I want to help her. I think... I think that's where my courage is coming from."

Saphina smiled, her wings shimmering in the sunlight. "Sometimes, the things we care about most are the very things that make us brave," she said. "Courage is often born from love and compassion. You are braver than you know, Linden."

Her words touched something deep within him, and he felt a warmth fill his heart. He was still scared, but he understood now that his fear didn't have to stop him. He could be afraid and still be brave, as long as he kept moving forward.

With a final look at his reflection, Linden stepped back from the pool, feeling a renewed sense of purpose. He thanked Saphina for her guidance, and they continued on their journey. The path grew steeper and more winding, and the trees around them began to tower higher, their branches weaving together like a thick canopy that blocked out most of the sunlight.

As they walked, Saphina pointed out small paths and hidden clearings, each one more mysterious than the last. Linden felt a mixture of awe and nervousness. The jungle felt alive in a way he hadn't noticed before, as if it were watching him, encouraging him to keep going.

They had been walking for what felt like hours when they came across a strange sight—a cluster of massive mushrooms growing in a perfect circle. Their tops were a bright shade of purple, and they seemed to glow faintly in the dim light.

"This is the Ring of Wisdom," Saphina explained, her voice soft with reverence. "It's said that those who stand in the center and speak their intentions aloud will find guidance in their journey. But be cautious, for the ring reveals truths that one must be ready to hear."

Linden felt a shiver run down his spine. The Ring of Wisdom looked both enchanting and intimidating, and he wasn't sure if he was ready to face whatever truths it might reveal. But he remembered Tovo's words about courage and decided to trust in the journey.

Slowly, he stepped into the ring, his paws feeling the cool earth beneath him. He closed his eyes and took a deep breath, feeling the quiet energy of the place surround him. "I am Linden," he said softly, his voice barely a whisper. "I am here to find the singing tree for my friend Penny, who has lost her voice. I am afraid, but I want to help her. I need guidance... and courage."

For a moment, there was only silence. Then, a gentle breeze swept through the ring, carrying with it the soft rustle of leaves. Linden felt a warmth spread through him, as though the jungle itself was responding to his words. In that moment, he felt a quiet sense of peace, a reassurance that he was not alone in his quest.

As he opened his eyes, he saw Saphina smiling at him from the edge of the ring. "The jungle has heard you, Linden," she said. "Trust in the path you're on. Every step you take brings you closer to finding the courage within yourself."

They continued on, the path becoming more challenging as they climbed over rocks and wove through thick underbrush. But Linden's heart was lighter now, filled with a sense of purpose that made the obstacles feel less daunting. He had asked for courage, and though he didn't know exactly how it would come, he trusted that it would be there when he needed it.

When they reached the edge of a steep hill, Saphina stopped and turned to him. "This is as far as I can guide you, Linden," she said, her voice filled with gentle encouragement. "The path beyond is one you must travel alone, but remember—you carry the strength of every step you've taken with you."

Chapter 5: Meeting Grizelda the Gorilla

Linden continued along the winding path, the jungle around him growing denser with each step. The tall trees blocked much of the sunlight, casting the forest in deep greens and mysterious shadows. Every sound seemed amplified—the rustle of leaves, the creak of branches, and the occasional distant call of an animal. It was a new part of the jungle for Linden, full of unknowns, and though he felt a twinge of fear, he reminded himself why he was here.

Ahead, the path suddenly opened into a small clearing, and Linden froze. Standing in the center of the clearing was a large, formidable figure—a towering gorilla with thick, dark fur and powerful arms. She was far larger than any creature Linden had encountered so far, and her presence alone made his heart race. Her gaze was fixed on him, unblinking and intense.

Linden's first instinct was to back away, but he remembered the courage he had been cultivating on his journey. He took a deep breath and held his ground, his paws trembling slightly.

"Who dares enter my part of the jungle?" the gorilla boomed, her voice deep and commanding.

Linden swallowed hard, feeling a shiver run down his spine. He didn't want to turn and run, but he wasn't sure how to respond to such a daunting figure. He took a steadying breath and replied, his voice softer than he had intended, "My name is Linden. I'm... I'm on a journey to find the singing tree."

The gorilla raised an eyebrow, studying him closely. Her eyes held a mixture of curiosity and amusement, as if she found the small, timid lion cub before her to be both puzzling and interesting.

"The singing tree, you say?" she asked, her tone less severe but still powerful. "And why would a little cub like you go searching for such a thing?"

Linden's heart pounded, but he stood a bit taller. "My friend Penny lost her voice, and I want to help her get it back. I heard the singing tree has the power to restore lost voices."

The gorilla tilted her head, her expression softening just slightly. She seemed to be considering his words, and after a long silence, she finally spoke. "I am Grizelda, guardian of this part of the jungle. Many creatures come and go, but few dare to approach me directly. Yet here you are, a young cub, standing in front of me with purpose."

Linden's ears perked up as he sensed a small glimmer of approval in her voice. He mustered his courage and asked, "Will you let me pass, Grizelda?"

Grizelda chuckled, a deep and rumbling sound that seemed to shake the ground beneath them. "Let you pass? That would be too easy," she said, crossing her powerful arms. "You say you're brave, but bravery is not shown just by words. I have a test for you, young one."

Linden's heart skipped a beat, and he felt his stomach twist. He wasn't sure what kind of test she had in mind, but he could tell it wouldn't be simple. Nevertheless, he nodded, determined to do whatever it took to continue on his journey. "What must I do?" he asked, his voice steady despite his nerves.

Grizelda gestured to a towering tree at the edge of the clearing. Its branches were high, and the bark was rough and thick. Hanging from one of the branches was a small fruit, bright orange and glistening in the sunlight. "If you are brave, then climb this tree and retrieve that fruit," she instructed. "It may seem like a simple task, but reaching that fruit will require both courage and determination."

Linden looked up at the fruit, feeling a pang of doubt. He had never climbed a tree so tall before, and the task seemed intimidating. But he reminded himself why he was doing this—not just to prove himself, but for Penny. Taking a deep breath, he walked toward the tree, feeling Grizelda's watchful eyes on him.

He reached up, pressing his paws against the rough bark. The tree felt solid beneath him, but as he looked up at the height he needed to climb, his confidence wavered. Still, he took a deep breath and began to climb, his small paws gripping the bark as he made his way up, slowly but steadily.

The first few feet were manageable, but as he climbed higher, the branches grew thinner and more difficult to grip. His heart raced, and he could feel his muscles beginning to tire. He glanced down, and the ground seemed far below, making his stomach twist with nervousness. For a moment, he considered turning back, but then he remembered Penny's silent, hopeful face. She was counting on him, and he couldn't give up.

With renewed determination, Linden continued upward, his focus narrowing to each branch, each small movement. He reached out, inching closer to the fruit, his heart pounding as he neared his goal. Finally, with a final stretch, his paw brushed against the orange fruit, and he managed to grip it tightly. Triumph surged through him as he carefully plucked it from the branch, holding it close as he began his descent.

The way down was just as challenging, and Linden had to take each step carefully. But when he finally reached the ground, he looked up at Grizelda, his heart swelling with pride. "I... I did it," he said, holding the fruit out to her.

Grizelda looked at him, a hint of a smile on her face. "Well done, Linden," she said, nodding approvingly. "You may be small, but your heart is strong. True courage lies in pushing through your fears, even when you feel like turning back. You have shown me that you possess this kind of bravery."

Linden felt a warmth spread through him at her words. He had been scared, but he had persevered, and now he understood that courage wasn't about never feeling fear—it was about moving forward despite it.

Grizelda accepted the fruit, examining it thoughtfully. "This fruit is special," she explained. "It is said to give strength to those who truly need it. I will return it to you, but only after I have seen that your heart is pure and your intentions are honest."

Chapter 6: The Wisdom of Ula the Owl

As the day wore on, Linden pressed forward, his heart brimming with a newfound confidence after his encounter with Grizelda. The jungle around him seemed to hum with life, and he found himself observing details he had previously missed—the vibrant colors of the flowers, the sounds of leaves rustling in the breeze, and the way light filtered through the dense canopy above.

Linden didn't know what lay ahead, but each step he took seemed to fill him with more purpose. He thought of Penny and the joyful songs she had once shared, and he felt a renewed determination to find the singing tree and bring her voice back. But even with his courage building, he knew he still had much to learn, and the jungle had many mysteries waiting for him.

As the afternoon sun began to dip lower in the sky, Linden came across an ancient tree, its trunk wide and gnarled, and its branches stretching high above him like the fingers of a wise elder. Perched on one of the branches was a figure with large, watchful eyes—a great horned owl, her feathers speckled with shades of brown and gray that allowed her to blend seamlessly into the bark.

The owl's gaze was steady and calm, and her presence exuded a quiet authority. Linden instinctively knew this was a creature of great wisdom, and he felt both humbled and curious. She looked down at him, her golden eyes flickering with a gentle light.

"Greetings, young lion," she said, her voice soft yet filled with an undeniable strength. "I am Ula, keeper of wisdom in this part of the jungle. What brings you here, far from the safety of your pride?"

Linden took a deep breath, gathering his thoughts. "My friend, Penny, has lost her voice," he explained. "I'm searching for the singing tree to help her get it back. Each step of this journey has been... challenging," he admitted, "but I feel I must continue."

Ula nodded, her eyes narrowing as she studied him carefully. "Your purpose is noble, and your journey is one that requires a heart full of courage. But courage alone is not enough, young one," she said, her voice carrying a weight that made Linden listen closely. "Wisdom is also necessary, for without it, one's bravery can lead to recklessness."

Linden tilted his head, intrigued by her words. "How do I gain wisdom?" he asked earnestly. "I want to help Penny, but I don't know if I have the wisdom needed for such a journey."

Ula smiled softly. "Wisdom is not something you simply gain all at once, Linden. It is gathered over time, through experience, patience, and understanding. But I can offer you some guidance for now, and perhaps it will serve you well along your path."

Linden's ears perked up as he listened intently, eager to absorb whatever advice Ula could share. The owl closed her eyes for a moment, as though reaching deep within herself, and then she spoke in a voice that seemed to resonate with the very trees around them.

"Remember, young one," she began, "not everything is as it seems in this jungle. Often, the answers you seek are hidden beneath the surface, requiring not just sight, but insight. Look beyond what is immediately in front of you and trust your instincts."

Linden nodded, committing her words to memory. "Look beyond what is in front of me," he repeated thoughtfully. It was a strange concept, but he knew he would find meaning in it along the way.

Ula continued, her gaze unwavering. "In the face of obstacles, remember to listen carefully—not just to words, but to silence as well. Silence speaks in ways that words cannot, and it is often in the quiet moments that the greatest wisdom is found."

Linden pondered her advice. The idea of listening to silence was unfamiliar, yet he sensed there was a profound truth in her words. He thought back to the quiet courage he had felt by the Reflection Pool and wondered if silence might indeed hold a wisdom he hadn't yet understood.

"Thank you, Ula," Linden said, his voice filled with gratitude. "I'll remember your words as I continue on my journey."

Ula inclined her head, her eyes softening. "One more thing, young lion," she added, her voice carrying a gentle warmth. "Do not fear asking for help when you need it. Strength lies not only in independence but also in knowing when to seek guidance. The jungle is vast, and sometimes, the best path is one walked together."

Linden felt a wave of warmth and relief wash over him. He had often felt the need to face his challenges alone, believing it to be a measure of his bravery. But Ula's words reminded him that true courage could also mean accepting the kindness and wisdom of others.

As he prepared to continue on his path, Ula extended one of her large wings, gesturing to a nearby thicket of dense foliage. "Ahead, you will encounter a grove filled with thorns and brambles," she said. "To navigate it, you will need patience and care. It is easy to rush through challenges, but in doing so, we often make mistakes. Remember, young one, that wisdom often grows in moments of stillness."

Linden nodded, feeling a deep respect for the owl's words. He thanked her once more, his heart filled with a sense of purpose and peace. Ula watched him go, her eyes shining with a quiet pride. She knew that the young lion had much to learn, but she also sensed the strength of his heart and the goodness of his spirit.

As Linden ventured forward, he thought about the advice Ula had shared. He was beginning to understand that courage wasn't just about facing fears but also about understanding the world and oneself in a deeper way. There was a quiet power in wisdom, a strength that could guide him as surely as his bravery.

Soon, he came upon the grove Ula had warned him about. It was dense with thorny bushes, their branches twisted and covered in sharp brambles that seemed to form a natural barrier. The path through the grove was narrow, with very little room to maneuver without brushing against the thorns. Linden paused, considering his options.

He could try to push through quickly, hoping to avoid the worst of the scratches, or he could move slowly and carefully, ensuring he didn't harm himself along the way. Remembering Ula's words about patience, he chose the latter, stepping carefully and deliberately.

The journey through the grove was painstakingly slow. Each step required focus and care, as even the slightest misstep could result in a scratch from the thorns. Linden's muscles ached from holding himself so still, and there were moments when he felt tempted to rush, to push through and be done with it. But each time the impulse arose, he remembered Ula's advice and held back, choosing to respect the pace the grove demanded.

At one point, Linden's paw got caught in a particularly thorny bush. He felt a sharp pain and instinctively wanted to yank his paw free, but he stopped himself, breathing deeply and carefully disentangling his paw instead. The process was slow, but he managed to free himself without injury.

After what felt like hours, he finally emerged from the grove, his fur ruffled and his muscles tired, but unharmed. A sense of accomplishment filled him as he looked back at the dense thicket he had navigated. He realized that his patience had not only kept him safe but had also helped him appreciate the importance of moving with intention, of valuing each step rather than rushing to the end.

Chapter 7: The Raging River and the Crocodile Guard

Linden moved forward, his heart feeling lighter and his mind filled with Ula's wisdom. He was beginning to understand that each encounter in the jungle offered not only a new challenge but also a valuable lesson. His courage was growing, not because he was fearless, but because he was learning how to be brave in ways he hadn't imagined.

The path soon led him to the sound of rushing water, a deep rumbling that grew louder with each step. As Linden emerged from the trees, he came upon a wide, powerful river. The water churned and foamed, crashing against rocks and sweeping past with a force that made him shiver. The river was wide and intimidating, its strong current warning him to be cautious. Linden paused at the riverbank, scanning for any sign of a way across.

Just as he was contemplating his options, a shadow moved on the other side of the river. A large, scaly figure rose from the water, revealing a massive crocodile. His scales were dark green, nearly blending with the water, and his eyes were sharp, piercing through the mist that rose from the river. The crocodile's presence was imposing, and Linden felt his heart race. He knew this creature commanded respect, and he instinctively took a step back.

The crocodile's gaze settled on him, and he let out a low rumble. "Who approaches my river?" the crocodile asked, his voice deep and resonant, carrying over the roar of the water.

"I am Linden," he replied, his voice trembling slightly but holding steady. "I am on a journey to find the singing tree. My friend Penny lost her voice, and I want to help her get it back."

The crocodile's eyes narrowed, studying Linden with a calculating gaze. "The singing tree, you say?" he murmured, his voice carrying a hint of both interest and caution. "Many seek it, but few are willing to face the trials that lie in wait. Crossing this river is no small task, young one."

Linden took a deep breath, feeling both fear and determination swell within him. "I know it won't be easy, but I am prepared to face whatever challenges come my way," he said, hoping his voice conveyed the resolve he felt.

The crocodile regarded him silently for a moment before nodding. "I am Kyro, the guardian of this river," he said. "No one crosses without proving their courage. If you wish to pass, you must first face a test. The river is wild and unpredictable, and its currents can easily sweep away the unwary. You will need more than bravery to cross; you will need balance, patience, and strength."

Linden's heart pounded as he listened to Kyro's words. The river was unlike any challenge he had faced so far, and he wasn't sure if he had the skills to make it across. But he knew he couldn't turn back now. He looked up at Kyro, his gaze steady. "I'll do my best," he said, his voice filled with determination.

Kyro tilted his head, a hint of approval in his gaze. "Very well," he replied. "But heed my advice. The river is not something to conquer; it is something to respect. Watch the water, learn its rhythms, and move with it. Fight it, and you will fail."

Linden nodded, his mind focused on Kyro's words. He approached the river's edge, feeling the cool mist from the water on his face. The river surged past him, its waves rising and falling in powerful swells. He took a deep breath, steadying himself before stepping into the shallow edge. The water was cold, and the force of the current pushed against his legs, reminding him of its strength.

Remembering Kyro's advice, Linden stood still for a moment, observing the river. He noticed that the waves seemed to come in a pattern, each swell rising and falling with a rhythm that pulsed like a heartbeat. He realized that if he timed his movements with the rhythm, he might be able to navigate through the waves without losing his balance.

Slowly, Linden began to wade deeper into the river, moving carefully and keeping his focus on the rhythm of the water. Each step required careful balance, as the current pushed against him, testing his strength. His paws slipped on the smooth rocks beneath him, and his muscles strained as he fought to stay upright. But he kept going, his mind fixed on each step, his determination unwavering.

At one point, a strong wave crashed against him, nearly knocking him off his feet. Linden stumbled, his heart pounding as he struggled to regain his balance. He remembered Kyro's words about respecting the river, and he took a deep breath, calming himself before taking another step. He adjusted his pace, moving with the flow rather than against it, and he found that the water seemed to ease its resistance.

Halfway across, he looked up to see Kyro watching him from the opposite bank, his gaze steady and approving. Linden felt a surge of encouragement, knowing that he was being tested not just by the river but by Kyro himself. He continued, step by step, focusing on each movement and refusing to let fear overwhelm him.

Finally, after what felt like an eternity, Linden reached the other side. His legs ached, and his fur was soaked, but he felt a powerful sense of accomplishment. He looked up at Kyro, his heart swelling with pride and gratitude.

Chapter 8: The Challenge of the Thistle Grove

The morning sun cast a golden glow over the jungle as Linden continued on his path, his steps steady and filled with purpose. The journey so far had been challenging, but each encounter had strengthened his resolve, and he felt his courage growing with every lesson learned. He knew that he still had much to face before reaching the singing tree, but he trusted in the wisdom he had gained from creatures like Grizelda and Kyro.

After walking for several hours, Linden came upon a new part of the jungle—a grove dense with towering thistle bushes and prickly vines that twisted and tangled in every direction. The thorns were sharp and plentiful, forming a natural barrier that seemed almost impenetrable. The sight was daunting, and Linden felt a pang of worry as he realized he would have to pass through this thorny maze to continue on his journey.

He took a deep breath, reminding himself of Kyro's advice to approach each challenge with patience and respect. He scanned the grove, looking for any potential path that might be less dense with thorns. After a few moments, he spotted a narrow opening between the bushes, and he carefully stepped forward, easing his way through the tight space.

The path was treacherous. Every step had to be calculated, every movement gentle, as even the slightest brush against the bushes would result in a scratch from the sharp thorns. Linden's fur was soon dotted with small red marks where the thorns had pricked him, and he winced as he moved forward, trying to avoid the most painful areas.

At one point, a particularly thick vine blocked his way, its thorns gleaming in the sunlight. Linden considered pushing through quickly, but he remembered Ula's lesson on patience and care. Instead of forcing his way, he crouched down, examining the vine closely to see if there was a way to navigate around it. With careful movements, he managed to slip beneath the vine without getting scratched, though his heart raced with each careful step.

As he moved deeper into the grove, Linden's muscles began to ache from the constant tension, and his fur was covered in small scratches. The thorns seemed to close in around him, forming a maze that tested both his patience and his resilience. He felt a surge of frustration, tempted to rush through and escape the painful barrier, but he reminded himself that impatience would only lead to more injuries.

"Take your time," he whispered to himself, drawing on the lessons he had learned. "Move with care."

His determination renewed, Linden continued on, each step careful and deliberate. He began to develop a rhythm, timing his movements to avoid the thorns as he twisted and turned through the grove. With each step, he felt a growing sense of accomplishment, knowing that he was making progress despite the challenge.

Just as he thought he was nearing the end, he encountered a dense patch of thistles that seemed impassable. The thorns were longer and sharper here, and the path was barely visible through the dense bushes. Linden's heart sank as he wondered if he had reached a dead end, but he took a deep breath, reminding himself of the patience and perseverance he had cultivated.

As he stood contemplating his options, he heard a soft, familiar voice from above. "Hello, young one. Having a bit of trouble?"

Linden looked up to see Saphina, the dragonfly who had guided him earlier in his journey, hovering above the thistle bushes. Her wings shimmered in the sunlight, and her bright eyes twinkled with kindness.

"Saphina!" Linden exclaimed, relief flooding through him. "This grove is so dense with thorns... I'm not sure how to get through."

Saphina nodded sympathetically. "The Thistle Grove is known for testing the patience and resilience of those who pass through," she said.

"But I see you've been moving carefully and thoughtfully. That is a good sign, Linden."

Linden sighed, his exhaustion evident. "I'm trying, but it's difficult. Every step feels like a challenge, and I can't rush through without getting hurt."

Saphina hovered closer, her voice soft and reassuring. "You're right, young one. This grove requires not only patience but also a calm mind. Rushing will only lead to pain, but if you take each step with intention, you'll find that the path becomes more manageable."

Linden listened closely, her words helping to steady his resolve. He took a deep breath, releasing the tension in his muscles, and reminded himself of his purpose. Penny's face flashed in his mind, and he felt a renewed determination to continue. With Saphina's encouragement, he pressed on, focusing on each step and moving slowly through the dense thistles.

As he navigated through the thickest part of the grove, Linden realized that the challenge was more than just physical. Each thorn, each twist in the path, tested his patience and self-control. He understood now that the Thistle Grove was a place of lessons, teaching him to move with mindfulness and respect for his surroundings.

After what felt like hours, he finally saw a small clearing ahead, the light filtering through the trees in soft rays that beckoned him forward. Linden's heart lifted, and he quickened his pace, carefully maneuvering through the last few thorny bushes until he emerged into the open space.

He took a deep breath, feeling the cool air on his scratched and sore fur. His muscles ached, and his paws throbbed, but he felt a profound sense of accomplishment. He had faced the Thistle Grove's challenge with patience and resilience, and he had come out stronger for it.

Chapter 9: Sariah the Snake's Clever Test

Linden ventured forward, feeling the effects of the day's journey in his tired legs and aching muscles. The jungle seemed to grow denser as he progressed, with shadows lengthening and strange sounds filling the air. As he moved along a winding path, he encountered a narrow opening between two tall trees. The air felt cooler here, and Linden noticed that the ground was covered in leaves that seemed untouched, as though few had dared to tread this path.

He continued carefully, his senses alert, when a sudden rustle from the leaves caught his attention. Before he could react, a sleek, emerald-green snake slithered out from the underbrush and coiled herself gracefully across the path in front of him. Her scales glistened in the filtered sunlight, and her eyes shone with an intense, knowing gaze.

Linden felt a shiver run down his spine. He'd heard stories about snakes in the jungle—some were kind, but others could be cunning and deceptive. Unsure of her intentions, he decided to approach with caution.

"Good day, young lion," the snake said in a voice that was as smooth as silk, her words almost a whisper. "I am Sariah, keeper of riddles and tests. And who might you be?"

Linden hesitated, choosing his words carefully. "My name is Linden," he replied. "I'm on a journey to find the singing tree. My friend Penny lost her voice, and I want to help her get it back."

Sariah tilted her head, her gaze thoughtful as she studied him. "The singing tree, you say? Quite an ambitious quest for such a young cub. Many have sought it, but not all have succeeded," she said, her voice holding a hint of intrigue. "To reach it, you must prove that you are not only brave but also clever."

Linden's heart pounded. He had faced physical challenges and tests of patience, but now it seemed he would have to use his mind to move forward. He wasn't sure if he was clever enough to meet Sariah's standards, but he knew he had to try.

"What do I have to do?" Linden asked, his voice steady despite his nerves.

Sariah let out a soft, amused hiss. "I will present you with a riddle," she replied. "Answer correctly, and I will allow you to pass. But beware—if your answer is wrong, you will find yourself lost, wandering in circles until you learn the wisdom you lack."

Linden swallowed hard, feeling the weight of her words. He took a deep breath, centering himself as he prepared to listen carefully to her riddle.

Sariah's eyes glinted as she began, her voice lilting with a rhythmic cadence. "I am something. I am fragile but strong, hidden yet seen. I connect yet divide, close but distant in between. What am I?"

Linden furrowed his brow, repeating the riddle in his mind as he searched for meaning. The words "fragile but strong" echoed in his thoughts. What could be both of these things? He thought of the delicate webs spiders spun, but he quickly dismissed the idea. A spider's web was not "close but distant."

His mind raced as he continued to analyze the riddle. "Hidden yet seen," she had said. Something that was not always visible but existed everywhere. His gaze drifted to the sky, where faint clouds floated, partially obscuring the sun. And then, suddenly, it came to him.

"Is the answer... a bridge?" he asked hesitantly. "A bridge connects but also separates, allowing passage yet marking a boundary. It can be fragile but strong, hidden from view but known to be there."

Sariah's eyes sparkled with approval. "Well reasoned, young cub," she said, her voice warm with praise. "A bridge, indeed. Many things connect us, yet there are boundaries that both unite and separate. You are wiser than you appear."

Linden felt a surge of pride, grateful for her recognition. He realized that courage wasn't just about physical strength or endurance; it was about using his mind and trusting in his ability to solve problems.

Sariah inclined her head, her movements fluid and graceful. "You may pass, young one," she said. "But before you go, I offer you another piece of wisdom."

Linden listened intently, eager to learn from her. Sariah's gaze softened, her eyes reflecting a depth of knowledge. "Remember that not all challenges require brute force or endurance. Some, like this riddle, are best approached with patience and thoughtfulness. In the jungle, as in life, the most powerful tool you have is your mind."

Linden nodded, absorbing her words. He was beginning to understand that each challenge on his journey was preparing him in a different way. He had learned patience from Grizelda, respect for nature from Kyro, and now, the importance of using his mind from Sariah.

He thanked Sariah, bowing his head respectfully before stepping past her. As he moved along the path, her riddle lingered in his mind. The idea of a bridge resonated with him, symbolizing the connections and boundaries he was discovering on his journey. He realized that each creature he encountered acted as a bridge of sorts, offering him wisdom that brought him closer to the singing tree and, ultimately, to Penny.

The path grew narrower as he ventured deeper into the jungle. The trees seemed to close in around him, their branches intertwining overhead to form a dense canopy that filtered the sunlight into scattered patches on the forest floor. Linden walked carefully, his mind alert and his senses attuned to the sounds and sights around him.

Just when he thought he was alone, he heard a faint rustling sound nearby. He paused, his ears perked up as he scanned the area. From the underbrush, a small figure emerged—a meerkat with a curious expression and bright, inquisitive eyes. She seemed to be studying him, her head tilted slightly as she observed him from a short distance.

"Hello," Linden said, offering a friendly smile. "My name is Linden. I'm on a journey to find the singing tree."

The meerkat's eyes widened with excitement. "The singing tree? You must be very brave!" she exclaimed. "My name is Marza. I've heard stories about the singing tree, but I never thought I'd meet someone who's actually searching for it."

Linden chuckled, feeling a sense of camaraderie. "It's been a challenging journey," he admitted. "But I've learned so much from everyone I've met along the way."

Marza nodded enthusiastically. "The jungle is full of lessons, and every creature has something to teach," she said, her voice filled with admiration. "I may be small, but I know that wisdom comes in many forms."

Her words reminded Linden of Sariah's riddle and the importance of using his mind. He realized that courage wasn't just about bravery in the face of fear; it was also about recognizing the strengths he carried within, even those that might not seem obvious at first.

Chapter 10: Encounters with the Mischievous Monkeys

As the first light of dawn crept into the sky, Linden awoke, stretching his tired limbs and feeling a renewed sense of purpose. His journey had been filled with challenges, each one shaping him in new and unexpected ways. With every step, he felt his confidence growing, and the thought of helping Penny spurred him forward. Today, as he set off, he felt a slight spring in his step.

The morning was warm, and as Linden walked along a winding path through the jungle, he marveled at the world around him. The lush greenery and colorful blossoms seemed to sparkle with morning dew, and the jungle was alive with the sounds of birds chirping, insects humming, and leaves rustling in the gentle breeze. Linden took a deep breath, feeling a sense of harmony with the jungle.

Suddenly, he heard an unusual rustling sound coming from the trees above. Startled, he looked up, but before he could make sense of what he saw, something small and round hurtled through the air, landing with a splat just inches from his paw. Linden jumped back, eyes wide in surprise as he saw a half-eaten piece of fruit lying on the ground.

"Got him!" a gleeful voice called from above, followed by a chorus of giggles. Linden squinted, trying to make out the shapes in the trees, and soon he spotted a group of monkeys, their eyes twinkling with mischief. They swung from branch to branch, chattering excitedly and tossing bits of fruit down at him.

Linden took a step back, not sure whether to laugh or feel annoyed. "Hey!" he called up to them. "Why are you throwing fruit at me?"

One of the monkeys, a small, brown-furred fellow with a cheeky grin, swung down to a lower branch, crossing his arms as he grinned at Linden. "We're just having some fun! You looked like you could use a little excitement," the monkey replied, his voice full of mischief.

Linden tilted his head, feeling his patience being tested. He remembered the many lessons he had learned on his journey—about patience from Grizelda, respect for nature from Kyro, and cleverness from Sariah. He took a deep breath, reminding himself to stay calm.

"I appreciate the excitement, but I'm on an important journey," Linden said, trying to keep his tone polite. "I'm looking for the singing tree to help my friend Penny, who has lost her voice."

The monkeys exchanged glances, their eyes widening with intrigue. "The singing tree?" one of the other monkeys, a gray-furred female, exclaimed, swinging down to join her friend. "That sounds like quite the adventure!"

The cheeky brown monkey leaned forward, his grin widening. "But if you're on such an important journey, shouldn't you be ready for a challenge?" he asked, mischief gleaming in his eyes. "We monkeys know all about bravery. Let's see if you're as brave as you say you are."

Linden felt his heart sink slightly, realizing that these monkeys were more interested in playfulness than seriousness. "What kind of challenge?" he asked cautiously, not entirely sure he wanted to play their games.

The monkey smirked, his tail curling mischievously. "It's simple," he said. "If you can catch one of us, we'll let you pass without any more fruit attacks. But if you can't, you'll have to dance with us up in the trees!"

The other monkeys burst into laughter and cheered, swinging from branch to branch, clearly enjoying the idea of their new game. Linden hesitated. He wasn't sure how chasing a monkey would help him on his journey, but he also didn't want to spend the rest of the day dodging flying fruit.

"Fine," he said, feeling a mix of determination and resignation. "I'll play along."

The cheeky brown monkey clapped his hands in delight. "Catch me if you can, then!" he called, leaping to a higher branch with remarkable agility.

Linden took a deep breath, his eyes narrowing as he focused on the monkey's movements. He crouched low, his body tense, watching as the monkey darted from branch to branch, taunting him with playful shrieks and giggles.

At first, Linden struggled to keep up, his eyes darting back and forth as the monkey led him in a dizzying chase. But as he followed, he began to notice a pattern in the monkey's movements. The monkey would pause on certain branches, always favoring those with sturdy limbs before leaping to thinner branches for a quick escape.

Drawing on the patience he had learned, Linden slowed down, conserving his energy and watching the monkey's rhythm closely. When the monkey paused on a thicker branch, Linden positioned himself just beneath it, timing his movements carefully.

With a sudden burst of speed, Linden leaped up, stretching his paw out toward the branch where the monkey was perched. The monkey, surprised by Linden's sudden accuracy, let out a startled squeak and tried to leap away, but Linden had anticipated the move. With a swift swipe, he tapped the monkey's tail, grinning as he landed gracefully on the ground.

"Got you!" Linden declared triumphantly.

The other monkeys erupted into cheers and laughter, clearly impressed by Linden's cleverness. The brown monkey looked at him, wide-eyed and slightly sheepish. "I have to admit, I didn't think you'd actually catch me," he said, a hint of respect in his tone.

Linden smiled, feeling a sense of accomplishment. "Sometimes, a little patience and observation go a long way," he said, echoing the lessons he had learned from Grizelda and Sariah. "Not everything is about speed."

The monkeys chattered excitedly, exchanging glances as they gathered around him. The gray-furred female stepped forward, her eyes twinkling with admiration. "You're braver and smarter than we thought," she said. "We've decided we like you. And as a reward for catching our fastest member, we'll help you on your journey."

Linden's curiosity was piqued. "How can you help?" he asked, intrigued by their offer.

The gray monkey grinned, pointing up into the dense canopy. "We know these trees better than anyone else," she said. "There's a shortcut just ahead, a hidden path through the trees that will take you closer to the singing tree. It's not easy to find, but we'll show you the way."

Linden's heart lifted with gratitude. "Thank you," he said sincerely. "That will be a huge help."

The monkeys formed a lively escort, guiding Linden through the maze of trees and vines with astonishing agility. They leaped from branch to branch, showing him the hidden pathways and narrow trails that wove through the dense jungle. Linden followed, feeling a renewed sense of excitement as they brought him closer to his destination.

As they traveled, the monkeys shared stories of their adventures in the jungle, filling the air with laughter and chatter. Linden found himself enjoying their company, realizing that their playful spirits and mischievous nature were balanced by a loyalty and kindness he hadn't expected. They may have been tricksters, but they were also fiercely protective of their jungle home and eager to help those they respected.

Finally, the monkeys brought him to a clearing where the path continued ahead, winding deeper into the jungle. They stopped, turning to face Linden with wide smiles and cheerful waves.

"This is as far as we go," the gray monkey said. "The singing tree lies further ahead. But be careful—there are challenges yet to come."

Linden replied, "Thank you, all of you," he said. "Your help means more to me than you know."

Chapter 11: Facing the Foggy Forest

The journey continued as Linden ventured deeper into the heart of the jungle. The path had become narrower and more winding, and the trees grew denser, their branches stretching out like twisted arms that cast long shadows on the ground. The air around him grew cooler, and a mist began to settle over the forest floor, curling around the trees in ghostly tendrils.

As he stepped forward, Linden felt a strange chill settle over him. The mist thickened until it was a dense fog, obscuring his vision. He could barely see his own paws, let alone the path in front of him. The trees around him faded into gray shadows, and every sound seemed muted, as though the fog were swallowing the very essence of the jungle.

Linden took a deep breath, steadying himself. He had learned so much on his journey so far, gathering wisdom from the creatures he met and finding courage he hadn't known he possessed. But now, in this foggy forest, he felt a twinge of uncertainty. Without his sight to guide him, he would have to rely on his other senses—and his instincts.

He took a cautious step forward, his paws brushing against the damp leaves scattered on the ground. The silence was almost eerie, broken only by the occasional rustling of leaves or the distant call of a bird. Linden reminded himself to stay calm. Ula's words echoed in his mind: "Remember, young one, that in silence, there is often wisdom."

Determined to press on, Linden moved slowly, each step deliberate as he tried to tune into the forest around him. The fog thickened further, wrapping around him like a soft, cold blanket. He could feel the dampness settling on his fur, and the path ahead seemed to disappear into the haze. Every now and then, he thought he saw shadows flickering at the edges of his vision, but whenever he turned, there was nothing there.

The stillness began to weigh on him, making him feel small and isolated. But he knew that turning back was not an option. He had come too far, and his friend Penny needed him. If he was to continue, he would need to trust his instincts more than ever before.

As he moved cautiously through the fog, Linden heard a faint sound—a soft, rhythmic whisper that seemed to come from all around him. He stopped, his ears straining to catch the noise. It was a gentle hum, like a distant melody carried on the breeze. Linden closed his eyes, focusing on the sound, allowing it to guide him forward.

Step by step, he followed the soft humming, letting it become his guide through the mist. His heart pounded in his chest, each beat a reminder of his purpose and his determination. The melody grew louder as he moved forward, filling the silence with a comforting rhythm.

Just as he felt the fog closing in around him, the faint outline of a figure appeared in the mist. Linden blinked, unsure if his eyes were playing tricks on him, but as he moved closer, the shape became clearer—a large owl perched on a low branch, her eyes gleaming through the fog.

"Ula!" Linden exclaimed, relief flooding over him. He was surprised to see her again, especially here, in the heart of the foggy forest.

Ula's eyes glinted with warmth and wisdom. "You are brave to venture this far, young one," she said, her voice soft yet strong. "The foggy forest is a place of tests. Here, one must trust not only their senses but also their heart."

Linden nodded, grateful for her presence. "It's hard to find the way forward when I can't see where I'm going," he admitted.

Ula tilted her head, her feathers rustling softly. "True vision does not come from the eyes alone," she said. "In places like this, you must rely on more than sight. You must trust your inner voice, the quiet strength within that guides you when all else fails."

Linden listened closely, letting her words sink in. He understood that this was more than just a lesson in navigation—it was a reminder to trust himself and his instincts, even when everything around him was uncertain.

"Close your eyes, young one," Ula instructed. "Listen to the forest, feel its rhythm, and let it guide you. The fog may obscure your vision, but it cannot silence the wisdom of the jungle."

Linden hesitated for a moment, then closed his eyes, his breathing slow and steady. He focused on the sounds around him—the faint rustle of leaves, the soft hum of distant insects, the gentle whisper of the wind as it moved through the trees. He could feel the pulse of the jungle, a steady rhythm that seemed to align with his own heartbeat.

With his eyes closed, Linden took a cautious step forward, then another, relying on the sounds and sensations around him. The fog still surrounded him, but he found that by trusting in the sounds and the feeling of the ground beneath his paws, he could move forward without fear.

Ula's voice floated through the fog, a steady presence guiding him. "The path to true courage is often unclear, but it is always within reach for those who listen to their hearts."

With each step, Linden felt his confidence growing. He realized that the fog, while intimidating, was not an obstacle; it was a teacher, encouraging him to trust himself. He understood that there would be times when the path ahead was obscured, but as long as he trusted in his own strength and the wisdom he had gathered, he could find his way.

After a few more careful steps, the fog began to thin, and Linden could see the faint outlines of trees and bushes emerging from the mist. He opened his eyes, blinking as his surroundings became clearer. The fog gradually lifted, revealing a sunlit clearing ahead.

Linden turned to thank Ula, but she was already gone, her presence fading back into the forest as quietly as she had arrived. He felt a pang of gratitude for her guidance, knowing that her words had helped him discover a new level of courage within himself.

As he stepped into the clearing, Linden felt a sense of accomplishment. He had faced the foggy forest not by fighting it, but by moving with it, allowing his instincts to guide him. The lesson he had learned was one of trust—trust in himself, in his abilities, and in the quiet wisdom that lay within.

The clearing was peaceful, with patches of wildflowers blooming in soft shades of purple and blue. Linden took a moment to rest, feeling the warmth of the sun on his fur as he reflected on his journey so far. He realized that every step he took brought him closer not only to the singing tree but also to a deeper understanding of himself.

Chapter 12: The Wise Words of Balthazar the Bear

As Linden moved forward, the trees began to thin, giving way to an open expanse that stretched out before him. It was a calm and quiet valley, filled with soft grasses and clusters of wildflowers that dotted the landscape with bursts of color. Linden felt a gentle breeze brush against his fur, carrying with it a sense of peace and stillness.

The valley seemed almost too peaceful, a stark contrast to the dense jungle he had navigated. But Linden's journey had taught him that places of beauty often held challenges of their own. He proceeded cautiously, his eyes scanning the area for any sign of what might come next.

As he ventured deeper into the valley, Linden's gaze fell upon a large figure resting in the shade of an ancient oak tree. The figure was a bear, massive and powerful, with thick, dark fur that shone in the sunlight. His eyes were closed, and his breathing was slow and steady, as though he were in a state of deep contemplation.

Linden approached carefully, unsure if he should disturb the bear. But as he got closer, the bear's eyes opened, revealing a pair of warm, intelligent eyes that seemed to hold a world of knowledge. The bear looked at Linden with a gentle curiosity, his expression both kind and wise.

"Greetings, young lion," the bear said in a deep, resonant voice that carried a sense of calm. "I am Balthazar, the elder of this valley. What brings you to these parts?"

Linden felt a surge of respect for Balthazar's presence, sensing that he was in the company of someone truly wise. "My name is Linden," he replied, his voice filled with reverence. "I'm on a journey to find the singing tree. My friend Penny lost her voice, and I want to help her get it back."

Balthazar nodded slowly, a look of understanding passing over his face. "Ah, the singing tree," he murmured, as though the name brought back old memories. "Many have sought it, but few have reached it. Your journey must be one of courage and purpose."

Linden nodded, feeling a deep connection to Balthazar's words. "I've learned a lot along the way," he said. "Every creature I've met has taught me something important, and each lesson has brought me closer to understanding what it means to be brave."

Balthazar studied him thoughtfully, a small smile tugging at the corners of his mouth. "Courage, young one, is not a single quality," he said. "It is a collection of virtues—strength, wisdom, resilience, and compassion—all working together to guide you."

Linden listened intently, eager to absorb Balthazar's wisdom. He could feel the weight of the bear's words settling within him, adding to the lessons he had already learned.

"Tell me, Linden," Balthazar continued, "what has this journey taught you about yourself?"

Linden thought for a moment, reflecting on his experiences. "I've learned that courage isn't just about facing danger," he said slowly. "It's about trusting myself, being patient, and learning from others. Each challenge has helped me grow, and I feel braver now than when I started."

Balthazar nodded approvingly. "You are wise beyond your years, young lion," he said. "But remember, true courage also means embracing the unknown. There will be times when you feel uncertain or afraid, and in those moments, you must hold on to the lessons you have learned."

Linden felt a warmth spreading through his chest, a feeling of strength and assurance that came from Balthazar's words. He realized that his journey was not only about finding the singing tree but also about discovering who he was and what he was capable of.

Balthazar shifted his position, his massive paws resting on the ground as he looked out over the valley. "In my younger days," he began, "I, too, sought the singing tree. I believed that its magic would grant me the strength I needed to protect my family and my home. But as I journeyed, I discovered that the strength I sought was already within me."

Linden listened, captivated by Balthazar's story. "Did you find the singing tree?" he asked, curiosity filling his voice.

Balthazar chuckled, a deep, rumbling sound. "I did not," he replied. "But the journey taught me more than any magical tree could have. I learned to trust in myself and my abilities, to find strength in my own heart rather than seeking it elsewhere."

Linden pondered this, understanding the wisdom in Balthazar's words. He realized that his journey was doing the same for him—helping him uncover the strength he already possessed.

Balthazar regarded him with a kind smile. "Remember, Linden," he said, "the journey itself is often as important as the destination. Each step you take, each lesson you learn, brings you closer to understanding the courage within you."

Linden nodded, feeling a deep gratitude for Balthazar's wisdom. "Thank you, Balthazar," he said sincerely. "Your words have given me a new perspective. I'll remember them as I continue on my journey."

Balthazar inclined his head, his eyes shining with pride. "You are welcome, young one. And remember, true courage also includes kindness. Never forget the importance of helping others along the way. The strength you find in yourself will be even greater when shared with others."

As Linden prepared to leave, Balthazar reached out a massive paw, placing it gently on Linden's shoulder. "Take this with you," he said, handing Linden a small, smooth stone. "It is a reminder that even the strongest mountains are shaped by time and patience. Let it remind you of the strength within you."

Linden accepted the stone, feeling the weight of its smooth surface in his paw. His heart was swelling with gratitude and determination. With a final look of thanks, he turned to continue his journey, carrying Balthazar's words and the stone as symbols of the strength and wisdom he had gained.

Chapter 13: Braving the Night in the Jungle

As the last light of day slipped beyond the horizon, the jungle around Linden transformed. Shadows grew long, blending together until the world was bathed in twilight. The once familiar sights of the trees and bushes became dark silhouettes, and the comforting sounds of daytime creatures were replaced by the eerie calls of the jungle's nocturnal inhabitants. It was the first time Linden had ventured so deep into the jungle at night, and he felt his courage wavering.

Despite the lessons he'd learned and the strength he had gained, a natural fear of the dark lingered within him. He reminded himself of why he was here, why he had come this far: to help his friend Penny. This purpose, though powerful, did little to calm his racing heart as the unfamiliar sounds filled his ears. He took a deep breath, steadying himself, and reminded himself of Balthazar's words: "True courage also includes kindness. Never forget the importance of helping others."

With each step, Linden walked more slowly, his senses heightened. The jungle, which had been a welcoming place of vibrant greens and cheerful animal calls during the day, felt entirely different under the cloak of night. The darkness made the trees look taller, their branches more twisted, and the faint rustling of unseen creatures felt amplified, echoing in the silence.

As he moved carefully, Linden noticed a pair of eyes gleaming in the darkness, reflecting the moonlight like two tiny lanterns. He froze, his heart pounding as he watched the eyes move closer, revealing the silhouette of a small fox with sleek, dark fur and a curious gaze. The fox approached him cautiously, her nose twitching as she sniffed the air around him.

"Who are you?" she asked in a voice that was soft and cautious.

"My name is Linden," he replied, trying to keep his voice steady. "I'm on a journey to find the singing tree to help my friend."

The fox tilted her head, her eyes studying him with a mixture of curiosity and respect. "A journey at night? That's a brave thing for a young lion," she remarked. "The jungle can be unpredictable in the dark."

Linden nodded, feeling a surge of courage rise within him. "I know. But I can't turn back now. I have to continue, even if it means facing the jungle at night."

The fox's gaze softened, and she offered him a small, understanding smile. "You have a good heart, Linden. My name is Selene, and I know these parts of the jungle well. Would you like some company on this part of your journey?"

Linden felt a wave of relief at her offer. "Thank you, Selene," he said gratefully. "I'd appreciate that."

Selene nodded, her presence calm and comforting as she led him along a narrow path through the trees. They walked in silence for a while, the only sounds being the soft rustling of leaves and the distant hoot of an owl. With Selene by his side, Linden felt a sense of peace settling over him, his initial fear of the night beginning to fade.

"The jungle changes at night," Selene said after a few moments. "It becomes a place of stillness and mystery, where creatures hide in the shadows, and the world feels larger, more open. But remember, darkness doesn't always mean danger. Sometimes, it is simply a place where light has yet to reach."

Linden pondered her words, realizing that he had been quick to fear the night simply because it was unfamiliar. "I hadn't thought of it that way," he admitted. "The dark felt... overwhelming. But now, with you here, it feels a little less frightening."

Selene smiled gently. "Fear often grows when we face things alone," she said. "But with someone by your side, even the darkest places become manageable. Remember that courage is not about never being afraid. It's about choosing to keep going, even when you feel that fear."

Linden nodded, feeling a new sense of purpose as they continued. With each step, he began to notice things he hadn't before—the silvery sheen of moonlight on the leaves, the soft glow of fireflies blinking in the air, and the delicate song of a night bird echoing through the trees. The jungle, he realized, was still alive and beautiful, even in the dark.

As they walked, Selene paused suddenly, her ears perking up as she looked toward a dense patch of bushes. Linden followed her gaze, squinting into the darkness. He could hear a faint whimpering sound, like a small creature in distress.

Without a second thought, Linden moved toward the sound, pushing through the bushes until he found a small, frightened rabbit tangled in a patch of thorny vines. The rabbit's fur was ruffled, and its eyes were wide with fear as it struggled to free itself.

"Hold still," Linden said gently, lowering his voice to soothe the rabbit. "I'll help you."

He carefully nudged the vines aside, using his paws to pull away the thorns that had snagged the rabbit's fur. The rabbit trembled, but as Linden continued his gentle work, it slowly calmed, its eyes fixed on him with a look of gratitude. Finally, Linden managed to free the last vine, and the rabbit hopped forward, shaking its fur with relief.

"Thank you," the rabbit said, its voice soft but full of appreciation. "I thought I'd be stuck there all night."

Linden smiled. "You're welcome. Are you alright?"

The rabbit nodded, looking up at him with admiration. "It was brave of you to help me, especially in the dark. Not many would have stopped."

Linden felt a warmth in his heart. "Sometimes, courage is about helping others, even when it's a little scary," he said, echoing Balthazar's words.

THE COURAGEOUS QUEST OF LITTLE LEO   53

The rabbit bowed its head in thanks before disappearing into the shadows, leaving Linden with a sense of pride and purpose. He knew that each act of kindness, each step of courage, was bringing him closer to the strength he sought within himself.

Selene watched him with approval, her eyes shining in the moonlight. "You did well, Linden. Acts of kindness, no matter how small, build courage that carries us through our darkest moments."

They continued their journey, the path winding deeper into the jungle. The night grew colder, and the sounds around them shifted, but Linden felt a growing confidence, his fear of the dark replaced by a quiet determination. He realized that the night was not something to be feared but rather a part of the jungle's natural rhythm, a time of rest and mystery.

As they walked, Selene shared stories of her own adventures in the jungle, tales of navigating through the night, of facing challenges that required both bravery and caution. Her voice was calm and steady, and her stories painted a picture of a jungle that was both wild and welcoming.

They finally reached the edge of a small clearing bathed in moonlight. Selene paused, turning to face him. "This is where I must leave you, Linden," she said, her voice filled with warmth and encouragement. "The path beyond leads to the edge of the jungle, and from there, you will be close to the singing tree."

Linden felt a pang of sadness, but he knew that Selene's guidance had been a precious gift. "Thank you, Selene," he said sincerely. "I'm grateful for your kindness and the wisdom you've shared."

Selene inclined her head, her eyes reflecting the gentle light of the moon. "Remember, young lion, the night is not something to fear. It is a time to listen, to reflect, and to find strength in silence. Your courage will carry you through, even when the path is unclear."

With a final nod, Selene turned and disappeared into the shadows, leaving Linden standing alone in the moonlit clearing. He took a deep breath, feeling the cool air fill his lungs, and looked up at the stars glittering in the night sky. The fear he had felt earlier had been replaced by a sense of calm and purpose. He understood now that courage was not about banishing fear but about moving forward despite it.

Chapter 14: The Enchanted Clearing

The first light of dawn painted the sky in soft hues of pink and orange as Linden awoke, stretching his limbs and feeling the warmth of a new day on his fur. The darkness of the previous night was a memory now, and he felt a renewed strength from the courage he had found in himself during those uncertain hours. Selene's wisdom echoed in his mind: "The night is not something to fear. It is a time to listen, to reflect, and to find strength in silence."

As he ventured forward, Linden noticed that the jungle was changing again. The trees grew taller, their branches forming a canopy that let only gentle patches of sunlight filter through. The sounds of the jungle seemed softer here, as though everything had quieted in respect for something sacred and ancient that lay just ahead.

Before long, Linden entered a clearing unlike any he had seen before. The ground was covered in vibrant moss that glowed faintly in the morning light, casting a soft, welcoming aura over the space. Flowers in every color dotted the clearing, their petals gently swaying in a breeze that carried a delicate, sweet scent. Linden felt an overwhelming sense of peace, as though the very air was filled with warmth and kindness.

At the center of the clearing stood a tree unlike any other in the jungle. Its trunk was wide and twisted, and its branches spread high and far, covered with leaves that shimmered like emeralds. Golden vines climbed its bark, winding their way to the highest branches. The tree seemed to radiate a gentle, magical light, as though it were alive with something beyond nature.

Linden took a step forward, his heart pounding with a mix of awe and anticipation. He felt drawn to the tree, sensing that it held something powerful, something ancient that had witnessed countless generations of jungle life.

"Welcome, young lion," a warm, melodic voice said, breaking the silence.

Linden looked around, searching for the source of the voice. At first, he saw no one, but then he realized that the voice seemed to be coming from the tree itself. The branches rustled gently, as though the tree were speaking directly to him.

"Are... are you the singing tree?" Linden asked, his voice barely more than a whisper.

"Yes," the tree replied, its voice rich and soothing. "I am the singing tree, keeper of the jungle's wisdom and the source of its song. Many have come seeking my gifts, but only those with true courage and pure intentions are granted what they seek."

Linden took a deep breath, his heart filling with gratitude and hope. "My friend Penny has lost her voice," he said, his voice steady but filled with emotion. "She used her voice to bring joy to others, and without it, the jungle feels... quieter. I've traveled far to find you, hoping that you can help her."

The singing tree seemed to sigh, its branches swaying gently. "I see the love and kindness in your heart, Linden," it said. "Your journey has tested you in many ways, and you have proven yourself worthy. But before I can grant your wish, there is one final lesson you must learn."

Linden felt a mixture of surprise and determination. He had faced so many challenges already, but he was ready for whatever this last test would bring. "I'm ready," he said, standing tall.

The singing tree's voice softened. "Courage is not only about facing challenges; it is also about understanding when to let go and accept help. For this final test, you must open your heart to something you may not expect."

As the tree's words hung in the air, a gentle mist began to form around the clearing, swirling around Linden and filling the space with a soft, magical glow. The mist thickened, and soon Linden could barely see the tree's shimmering branches. But he wasn't afraid; he trusted in the singing tree's wisdom and waited patiently.

Suddenly, the mist parted, and Linden found himself looking at a figure standing at the edge of the clearing—a lioness, her fur a beautiful shade of gold, with a gentle, wise expression. She looked at him with kind, knowing eyes that held a depth of experience and compassion. Linden's heart leapt as he recognized her.

"Mother?" he whispered, his voice filled with surprise.

The lioness smiled, her eyes full of warmth and love. "Yes, my dear Linden," she replied. "I am here to help you with this final lesson."

Linden felt a mixture of joy and confusion. He had thought he was on this journey alone, but now his mother was here, and her presence filled him with comfort and strength. He took a step toward her, feeling as though he were a young cub again, seeking the warmth of her embrace.

His mother looked at him with a gentle smile, her gaze filled with pride. "Linden, your journey has been one of bravery and kindness. You have shown courage in ways that few could imagine. But there is one more thing you must understand: true courage sometimes means opening yourself to others, allowing them to share your burdens."

Linden listened, her words resonating deeply within him. He had been so focused on being strong and courageous for Penny that he hadn't considered that he, too, could rely on others for support.

"You are strong, my son," his mother continued, her voice soft and soothing. "But even the strongest hearts need companionship. True courage is not just about facing challenges alone; it's also about trusting others to be there for you."

Linden felt tears prickling at the corners of his eyes as he absorbed her words. He realized that he had been carrying the weight of this journey on his own, trying to prove himself by facing every challenge alone. But his mother's presence reminded him that he didn't have to bear everything by himself.

"Thank you, Mother," he said, his voice filled with emotion. "I understand now. I've been so focused on helping Penny that I forgot that sometimes, accepting help is part of being brave."

His mother nodded, her gaze filled with love. "And Penny's joy will be greater because of the love and support you offer, just as your courage has grown because of those who have helped you along the way."

The mist began to lift, and Linden felt his mother's presence fading, though her words lingered in his heart like a gentle warmth. He looked up at the singing tree, his heart filled with a newfound understanding of courage and connection.

"You have passed the final test, Linden," the singing tree said, its voice soft and approving. "Your heart is open, and your courage is complete. You have shown bravery, compassion, and humility. You are ready to receive the gift you seek."

With a gentle rustling, the tree lowered one of its branches, offering Linden a single, radiant leaf. The leaf glowed with a soft, golden light, filling the clearing with warmth. Linden took it carefully, feeling the power and beauty of the leaf in his paw.

"This leaf holds the song of the jungle," the singing tree explained. "When you give it to Penny, it will restore her voice, and the joy she brings will be even greater for all that you have shared."

Linden's heart swelled with gratitude. He bowed his head respectfully. "Thank you," he said, his voice filled with reverence. "I will cherish this gift and remember everything I have learned along the way."

Chapter 15: The Return Journey

With the glowing leaf from the singing tree carefully secured by his side, Linden began his journey back home. His heart felt lighter than it had since the start of his adventure, and he couldn't wait to see Penny again and restore her voice. The path back through the jungle was familiar, but now it held a new significance, each step a reminder of the lessons he had learned.

As he walked, Linden thought back to all the creatures who had helped him along the way—Grizelda the gorilla, Kyro the crocodile, Ula the wise owl, Saphina the dragonfly, Balthazar the bear, and Selene the fox. Each encounter had taught him something unique, shaping his understanding of courage, patience, wisdom, and kindness.

The jungle seemed to welcome him as he made his way through. The dense greenery felt less intimidating, the sounds more harmonious, and the shadows less mysterious. He felt as though he was seeing everything with new eyes, with a deeper appreciation for the beauty and interconnectedness of the world around him. It was a reminder of how much he had grown, not just in courage but also in understanding and compassion.

The morning passed quickly, and as the sun rose higher, Linden reached a familiar part of the jungle—a wide river he had crossed earlier in his journey. He remembered Kyro's advice to move with the flow, to respect the strength of the river instead of trying to fight it. Now, with the singing tree's gift in his possession, he felt even more prepared to face the river's currents.

As he stood at the riverbank, a familiar voice rumbled behind him. "Well, if it isn't the young lion on his way back home," Kyro said, his scaly figure emerging from the shade of a large tree. His sharp eyes glinted with approval. "I see you've made it to the singing tree."

Linden smiled, his heart swelling with gratitude. "Yes, Kyro," he replied. "Thank you for your guidance. It helped me more than you know."

Kyro nodded, a hint of a smile on his normally stern face. "You've proven yourself worthy, young one," he said. "Crossing the river requires patience and respect, but I can see you've learned even more than that."

Linden felt a surge of pride, but he also knew there was no need to boast. His journey had been about growth and understanding, and the wisdom he had gained was enough. "Would you help me cross again?" he asked, looking at Kyro with trust and respect.

Kyro nodded and positioned himself in the river, creating a safe path for Linden to navigate across. As Linden moved carefully over the rocks and shallow parts of the river, he kept Kyro's earlier advice in mind, moving with the rhythm of the water and allowing its flow to guide him.

Once he reached the other side, Linden looked back at Kyro with gratitude. "Thank you again, Kyro. I'll always remember the lessons you taught me."

Kyro simply nodded, his gaze proud yet serene. "Farewell, young one," he said. "May your courage continue to grow." With that, he disappeared into the river, his powerful form blending seamlessly with the water.

Linden continued on, his heart full. Each familiar path reminded him of the creatures who had helped him, each step strengthening his resolve to reach Penny and restore her voice. As he ventured further, the path led him back to the grove where he had first encountered Grizelda, the powerful and wise gorilla who had tested his patience and resilience.

To his delight, Grizelda was waiting for him at the edge of the grove. She looked at him with a knowing smile, her massive arms crossed as she observed his approach. "Well, if it isn't the brave little lion," she said, her voice filled with warmth and pride. "It seems you've returned from your journey victorious."

Linden nodded, his heart swelling with gratitude. "Thank you, Grizelda. Your test taught me so much about patience and determination."

Grizelda let out a hearty laugh. "You've proven yourself to be more than just a brave cub. You've grown wiser, and I can see that you carry the jungle's wisdom with you. Remember, young one, true strength lies not only in muscle but in the courage of the heart."

Linden bowed his head in respect, her words resonating deeply with him. "I won't forget," he promised.

Grizelda nodded approvingly, her gaze warm. "Go on now. You have a friend waiting for you," she said, motioning for him to continue on his journey.

With a grateful nod, Linden continued, the grove behind him as he ventured further toward home. His steps were confident, his heart full of the wisdom he had gathered. But as he walked, he felt a growing anticipation to see Penny again, to share with her the gift of the singing tree and the journey he had undertaken for her.

As the sun began to dip lower in the sky, Linden arrived at the edge of the jungle, where he spotted a familiar flash of blue and green feathers. Penny was perched on a low branch, her eyes bright as she spotted him. Linden's heart leapt with joy as he saw her, and he rushed forward, calling her name.

"Penny!" he exclaimed, his voice filled with excitement.

Penny turned, her expression lighting up with surprise and happiness as she saw him. She opened her beak as if to call his name but stopped, her eyes reflecting the sadness that lingered from her lost voice. Linden could see the struggle in her expression, the pain of being unable to share her joy with him.

But Linden smiled, feeling the weight of the singing tree's gift beside him. "Penny, I have something for you," he said softly, reaching for the glowing leaf that he had carried so carefully.

Penny watched in awe as he held out the leaf, its soft golden light casting a gentle glow over them. "This is a gift from the singing tree," Linden explained, his voice filled with emotion. "It holds the jungle's song, and it will restore your voice."

With a look of gratitude and wonder, Penny leaned forward, her eyes filling with tears as she took the leaf gently in her beak. The moment she touched it, a warm light enveloped her, filling the air with a soft, harmonious melody. The jungle seemed to hold its breath, the world growing quiet as Penny's voice returned, her song rising like the morning sun.

Penny sang a joyful, grateful melody that echoed through the trees, her voice bright and clear, filled with the love and warmth she had longed to share. The song was beautiful, a blend of joy and gratitude, and Linden felt his heart swell with pride and happiness as he listened.

As Penny's song filled the jungle, creatures began to gather, drawn by the beauty of her voice. Birds, squirrels, rabbits, and even Grizelda and Kyro appeared, their expressions filled with admiration and joy. Penny's song flowed over them like a river, filling the jungle with harmony and light.

When her song ended, Penny looked at Linden, her eyes shining with gratitude. "Thank you, Linden," she said, her voice filled with emotion. "Your courage, your kindness... it's because of you that I can sing again."

Linden felt a warmth fill his heart. "It was for you, Penny," he replied, his voice soft. "You bring joy to everyone, and the jungle wouldn't be the same without your song."

The creatures around them shook their heads in agreement, each one touched by the beauty of Penny's restored voice and the bravery of

Linden's journey. Grizelda, Kyro, and even Selene appeared from the shadows, each offering Linden a nod of respect.

Chapter 16: The Celebration of Song

Word spread quickly through the jungle that Penny's voice had returned, and soon creatures from all corners of the forest gathered to celebrate. From small insects to towering trees, every part of the jungle seemed alive with excitement, as if the land itself was rejoicing in the return of its beloved melody. The birds perched on high branches, squirrels chittered with joy, and even the usually shy animals came out of hiding to join in the celebration.

Linden stood beside Penny, feeling a warmth in his heart as he watched her bask in the happiness surrounding her. Penny's voice was more vibrant and beautiful than ever, her song a blend of joy, gratitude, and love. She glanced at Linden with shining eyes, and he felt a wave of pride and humility at what they had accomplished together.

"Linden," Penny said softly, leaning close so he could hear her over the sounds of the gathering animals. "Thank you doesn't feel like enough. You gave me more than my voice back—you gave me hope, friendship, and a reminder of all the beauty in the world."

Linden's heart swelled with emotion, and he shook his head modestly. "You would have done the same for me, Penny," he replied, his voice filled with sincerity. "Your voice brought joy to all of us, and the jungle felt different without it. I only did what I felt was right."

As the sun dipped lower in the sky, casting a warm, golden glow over the gathering, Grizelda the gorilla stepped forward, her powerful form towering over the group. She raised her arms, her deep voice commanding attention. "Friends, today we celebrate not only the return of Penny's song but also the courage and kindness of young Linden, who embarked on a journey through the heart of the jungle to help his friend."

The crowd erupted in cheers, their voices filling the air with a harmony that resonated deep within Linden. He felt a surge of gratitude and pride, though he kept his head bowed respectfully.

Grizelda continued, her gaze warm as she addressed the crowd. "Linden faced many challenges along the way—he met with obstacles that would have tested even the strongest of us. Yet he remained humble, patient, and true to his purpose. His journey has reminded us of the power of kindness and the strength we find when we work together."

Kyro, the wise crocodile, added his voice to the praise. "The courage Linden showed was not just in his heart but in his actions," he rumbled, his voice steady and proud. "He moved with respect for the jungle, learning from each challenge and showing all of us that true bravery includes humility and wisdom."

Linden looked around, his heart racing with gratitude. He felt overwhelmed by the kindness and respect being shown to him. He had set out simply to help his friend, yet here he was, surrounded by animals who looked at him with admiration. He realized that his journey had changed not only him but also those he had encountered, each one contributing to the strength and wisdom he now carried.

Penny stepped forward, her voice carrying a melody that softened the air around them. "Linden's bravery brought me back to my voice," she said, her tone gentle yet strong. "But it also reminded me of the courage it takes to rely on those we love. None of us is meant to face the world alone, and Linden's journey has shown us the beauty of supporting one another."

As Penny spoke, Saphina the dragonfly flitted down, her wings glistening in the fading sunlight. "Linden, you've taught us that patience and care can guide us through even the trickiest paths," she said, her voice full of admiration. "You reminded us all to look deeper, to move thoughtfully and considerately."

Linden smiled at her, remembering the many lessons she had imparted with her gentle guidance. The gratitude he felt was boundless, knowing that each creature had played an important role in shaping the courage he now held.

Ula the owl swooped down gracefully, her feathers shimmering as she perched on a low branch near the center of the gathering. Her wise eyes regarded Linden with warmth. "Young lion, your journey has shown us the importance of listening, not just with our ears but with our hearts," she said, her voice calm and steady. "You taught us that even in the darkest moments, we can find our way if we trust ourselves and those who offer us guidance."

Balthazar the bear lumbered forward, his deep, comforting voice adding to the chorus of praise. "Linden, your journey was not just about courage," he said. "It was about kindness, resilience, and the ability to face challenges with a heart full of compassion. You have shown us all that true strength is not measured in muscle but in the courage to help others and remain humble."

The animals cheered, their voices blending into a harmonious chorus that echoed through the jungle. Linden looked around, feeling a profound sense of belonging and unity. He realized that his journey had indeed been a gift—not only for Penny but also for himself and everyone he had encountered. He had learned that courage was not a solitary path; it was woven from the strength, wisdom, and kindness of everyone around him.

As the celebration continued, Penny began to sing, her voice rising like a river of light, filling the air with a melody that spoke of joy, love, and the beauty of friendship. The animals joined in, each one adding their own unique sound to the song, creating a symphony that echoed through the jungle.

Linden felt tears prickling at his eyes as he listened to the harmony of voices around him. He had never felt so connected to the jungle, to his friends, and to the world around him. Every voice, every creature, and every sound was a reminder of the journey he had taken and the strength he had found within himself.

When the song ended, the jungle grew quiet, the silence filled with the warmth of shared gratitude. Grizelda approached Linden, placing a

THE COURAGEOUS QUEST OF LITTLE LEO

gentle paw on his shoulder. "Linden, you have shown all of us the true meaning of courage," she said softly. "Your journey may have ended, but the lessons you have brought back will continue to inspire us all."

Kyro replied, "You remind us that courage is not a destination; it is a journey we continue every day, choosing to help, to learn, and to grow."

Linden had set out to restore Penny's voice, but he had returned with so much more—understanding, friendship, and a deep sense of connection to the jungle and its creatures. His heart was full, and he knew that the courage he had found would stay with him, guiding him through life's challenges.

Chapter 17: The Gift of Gratitude

The jungle gradually returned to its peaceful rhythm. The animals went back to their daily lives, but a sense of joy lingered in the air, as if Penny's song had left a lasting melody in every heart. Linden, too, felt the jungle's newfound harmony. He was grateful for all the experiences, lessons, and friendships his journey had brought him. Yet, he realized that one thing remained: he wanted to express his gratitude to each of his friends individually.

One morning, Linden rose early, deciding that his next adventure would be to thank every creature who had guided him, taught him, and supported him along the way. With Penny's blessing and encouragement, he set out, his heart filled with appreciation and a sense of purpose.

The first friend on his list was Grizelda, the wise gorilla who had tested his patience and resilience in the beginning. Linden made his way to the grove where he had first met her, the path now familiar and welcoming. When he reached the clearing, Grizelda was waiting, her tall frame silhouetted against the rising sun.

"Grizelda," Linden said, bowing his head in respect. "I came to thank you. Your lessons on patience and strength have guided me throughout my journey, helping me through the toughest moments. I wouldn't be who I am now without your wisdom."

Grizelda's face softened, her eyes filled with warmth. "Linden, the strength and patience were always within you," she replied gently. "I merely helped you recognize them. Remember, young lion, that wisdom and resilience are gifts that grow with each experience."

Linden nodded, feeling her words settle into his heart. "Thank you, Grizelda," he said, his voice full of sincerity. "Your guidance will stay with me forever."

With her blessing, Linden continued on, following the path that led to the river where he had met Kyro, the formidable crocodile. He could hear the sound of rushing water as he approached, the river flowing steadily under the morning light. Kyro was lounging on the riverbank, his sharp eyes watching Linden with a look of calm interest.

"Good morning, Kyro," Linden greeted him, stepping close to the river's edge. "I came to thank you for the lessons you taught me about respect and patience. Your guidance helped me understand how to move with the challenges, rather than against them."

Kyro gave a slow nod, his gaze thoughtful. "Respect for the journey is as important as courage, young lion," he replied. "Remember that every river, every path, has its own rhythm. When you listen to it, you'll find the way forward becomes clearer."

Linden smiled, grateful for Kyro's wisdom. "Thank you, Kyro. I'll carry your words with me always."

With a final nod, Linden left the river, feeling a renewed appreciation for the friends who had helped him. His next stop was Ula the owl, whose wisdom and insight had guided him through the foggy forest, teaching him the importance of trusting his inner voice. Linden followed the familiar path to the tree where Ula often perched, her wise eyes watching the jungle below.

As he approached, Ula tilted her head, a soft hoot escaping her beak. "Linden, it is good to see you again," she said, her voice calm and soothing. "What brings you here?"

"I came to thank you, Ula," Linden said, his voice filled with respect. "Your guidance helped me learn to trust myself, even in the face of uncertainty. Without your wisdom, I might not have found my way through the darkest parts of the journey."

Ula's eyes softened, and she nodded approvingly. "The wisdom was always within you, young one," she replied. "Sometimes, we need only a gentle reminder to listen to it. Remember, Linden, that even in the most challenging times, your inner voice will guide you."

Linden bowed his head, feeling her words settle deep within his heart. "Thank you, Ula. I'll always remember to listen."

With Ula's blessing, he continued on, each step filling him with a deeper sense of gratitude. His next stop was the grove where he had first encountered Saphina the dragonfly, whose gentle guidance had shown him the importance of patience and mindfulness. As he entered the grove, Saphina flitted over to him, her wings shimmering in the sunlight.

"Linden!" she exclaimed, her voice bright with delight. "It's wonderful to see you!"

"I came to thank you, Saphina," Linden said with a warm smile. "Your lessons taught me to move thoughtfully, to observe, and to trust in the wisdom around me. You showed me that courage doesn't always mean rushing forward; sometimes, it means moving with care."

Saphina's wings fluttered with pleasure, her eyes shining. "You learned well, young lion," she said kindly. "Patience and mindfulness are strengths that will guide you far. Remember, the smallest actions can hold the greatest power."

Linden nodded, feeling her words resonate within him. "Thank you, Saphina. I'll carry your lessons with me always."

As he left the grove, Linden felt a renewed sense of purpose, knowing that each friend had added something valuable to his journey. His heart was full, and he realized that gratitude was its own form of courage—acknowledging the impact others had on him with humility and respect.

His final stop was the clearing where he had met Balthazar, the wise bear who had taught him the importance of kindness and the courage to accept help. The gentle giant was resting beneath a large tree, his eyes closed as if in peaceful reflection.

"Balthazar," Linden called softly, not wanting to startle him.

The bear opened one eye, a smile spreading across his face as he saw Linden. "Ah, young lion," he rumbled. "It's good to see you again. What brings you here?"

"I came to thank you, Balthazar," Linden said, his voice filled with emotion. "You taught me that courage isn't just about strength. It's also about kindness, and about knowing when to accept help from others."

Balthazar nodded, his gaze warm and approving. "You have a heart filled with courage, Linden," he said softly. "The kindness you show others will always come back to you, strengthening the bonds that unite us all. Remember, true courage is as much about kindness and compassion as it is about facing challenges."

Linden bowed his head, deeply moved by Balthazar's words. "Thank you, Balthazar. Your wisdom has changed me, and I'll remember it always."

With a gentle nod and a reassuring smile, Balthazar raised a paw in a gesture of farewell. Linden felt a profound sense of closure as he left the clearing. He had come full circle, returning to each friend who had been part of his journey and expressing his gratitude. Each friend had contributed a piece of wisdom that, together, formed the strong, resilient courage he now carried within himself.

Chapter 18: The New Path Forward

One crisp morning, Linden sat beside Penny's tree, watching the light filter through the leaves. Penny was nearby, perched on a branch and humming softly to herself, her voice like a gentle breeze that filled the air with warmth. Her song had become a cherished part of the jungle once more, and every creature seemed to find peace in its melody.

As he sat, Linden found himself contemplating his journey and all that he had learned. His heart was full, yet he felt a pull—a quiet curiosity stirring within him, as if calling him to explore new horizons. He wasn't sure what it meant, but he sensed that his story wasn't over. The jungle, vast and filled with wonders, seemed to hold endless possibilities.

Penny noticed the far-off look in his eyes and tilted her head, studying him thoughtfully. "Linden, is something on your mind?" she asked, her voice filled with warmth and understanding.

Linden took a deep breath, feeling the weight of his thoughts. "I don't know, Penny," he replied slowly. "I just feel... drawn to something new. My journey to help you was so full of challenges, lessons, and friendship, and now that it's over, I wonder what else might be waiting for me out there."

Penny nodded, a knowing smile on her face. "Sometimes, the end of one journey is just the beginning of another," she said. "You've grown so much, Linden, and your heart is open to the world. Perhaps there are new adventures, new friends, and new lessons waiting for you."

Linden pondered her words, feeling a sense of excitement mixed with a hint of uncertainty. "Do you really think there's more for me to discover?" he asked, his eyes reflecting a spark of hope.

Penny chuckled softly. "The jungle is wide and full of mysteries," she replied. "Every corner holds something new to learn, and every creature has its own story to tell. You've already proven that you have the courage to face challenges and the heart to form connections. Who knows what wonders you might find?"

Linden felt his heart swell with excitement. He had always loved the jungle, but now, after his journey, he felt ready to explore it with new eyes. The world seemed brighter, larger, and more inviting, and he was filled with a desire to discover everything it had to offer.

At that moment, a soft rustling sounded from behind them, and Linden turned to see a young meerkat with bright, curious eyes and a small bundle of leaves. The meerkat paused, his gaze shifting between Penny and Linden with a look of admiration.

"Excuse me," the meerkat said, his voice a bit timid but full of respect. "Are you Linden? The one who went on the journey to find the singing tree?"

Linden smiled, nodding. "Yes, that's me," he replied, his voice warm and welcoming. "What can I do for you?"

The meerkat's eyes sparkled with excitement. "I've heard so much about your journey! The courage you showed, the friends you made... it's all so inspiring!" He hesitated, then held out the bundle of leaves. "I brought this as a gift, to thank you for everything you've done for the jungle."

Linden accepted the gift with gratitude, touched by the young meerkat's kindness. "Thank you," he said, his voice filled with appreciation. "It means a lot to me."

The meerkat's gaze was filled with awe. "Do you think... maybe... I could learn to be brave like you?" he asked shyly, his eyes wide with hope.

Linden's heart softened, and he placed a comforting paw on the meerkat's shoulder. "Of course," he said gently. "Bravery isn't about being fearless; it's about choosing to keep going, even when things seem difficult or uncertain. Just remember to be patient with yourself and to trust in the friends you make along the way."

The meerkat's face lit up, and he nodded eagerly, his tail twitching with excitement. "Thank you, Linden! I'll remember that!" With a final wave, he scampered off, his steps light with newfound confidence.

Penny watched him go, a smile on her face. "See, Linden?" she said softly. "Your courage has become a source of strength for others. You're a part of something bigger now, a story that's inspired others to find their own bravery."

Linden felt a warmth spread through him, realizing that his journey had indeed created ripples, touching the lives of others in ways he hadn't expected. He understood now that courage was something that grew and expanded, a force that connected him to everyone around him.

As the day wore on, Linden and Penny wandered through the jungle, visiting familiar places and greeting the friends they met along the way. The jungle seemed more vibrant, filled with laughter, warmth, and a sense of unity that Linden felt honored to be a part of.

At one point, they came across Selene, the fox who had guided Linden through the night. She was sitting by a small pond, her reflection shimmering in the water as she looked up and smiled warmly at them.

"Linden," Selene greeted him, her voice soft and kind. "It's good to see you again. I hear the jungle is full of stories of your journey."

Linden smiled, feeling humbled. "I owe so much of it to friends like you, Selene," he replied. "Your guidance that night taught me to trust in myself, even when the path wasn't clear."

Selene nodded, her eyes shining with pride. "And now you've become a beacon for others, helping them find their own courage. Remember, Linden, the heart that guides others grows even stronger with each new connection it makes."

They continued walking, Linden feeling a sense of purpose growing within him. His journey had taught him many things, and now he realized that sharing those lessons, helping others find their own paths, was the next part of his story. He wasn't just a cub who had gone on an adventure; he was a part of the jungle's tapestry, connected to every creature through the bonds of courage, kindness, and love.

Chapter 19: The Great Jungle Council

A few days after his journey of gratitude, Linden awoke to the sounds of excited chatter throughout the jungle. Birds called to one another, animals scurried from tree to tree, and a sense of eager anticipation filled the air. Curious, Linden made his way through the forest toward the source of the commotion, following a trail of animals who seemed to be gathering in one central place.

As he rounded a bend in the path, he came upon a vast clearing that was filled with creatures of all shapes and sizes. From tiny insects to towering elephants, every corner of the jungle was represented. At the center of the clearing stood a large stone that had long been used for important gatherings, and on top of it, Grizelda the gorilla was standing tall, her presence commanding and dignified.

Linden was puzzled. It had been a while since the jungle had seen a gathering of this size, and he couldn't help but wonder what could have brought everyone together. He moved closer, finding a spot among the crowd where he could see Grizelda clearly. Beside her stood Kyro the crocodile, Balthazar the bear, and Ula the owl, each one representing a different part of the jungle.

Grizelda raised her arms, calling for silence. The jungle quieted, and every creature turned their attention to her, their eyes filled with curiosity.

"Friends, thank you for gathering here today," Grizelda began, her deep voice carrying through the clearing. "We have called this council to celebrate a new era in our jungle. Over time, we have all learned that courage, kindness, and unity make us stronger. And today, we are here to honor someone who has embodied these values and brought us closer as a community."

Linden felt a twinge of surprise, realizing that the council was in part because of him. He looked around, seeing animals smile and nod in his direction, their expressions filled with warmth and admiration.

Grizelda continued, her gaze settling on Linden with pride. "Linden, you have shown us that courage is more than facing fears; it is about acting with kindness, seeking wisdom, and being open to others. Your journey to find the singing tree, and your efforts to help your friend Penny, have left a mark on all of us. Today, we gather to honor you and to share in the lessons you've brought back to the jungle."

A murmur of agreement spread through the crowd, and Linden felt a wave of humility wash over him. He hadn't set out to receive praise; he had only wanted to help his friend. Yet seeing the impact of his actions on those around him filled him with gratitude and a renewed sense of purpose.

Kyro stepped forward, his powerful form reflecting strength and calm. "Young lion," he said, his voice steady and thoughtful, "your journey taught us the importance of respecting the natural flow of things. Like the river that flows with purpose, you moved forward with respect and patience, learning to adapt to each challenge. Today, I ask you to share your wisdom with all of us."

Linden took a deep breath, his heart racing as he looked out at the gathered animals. Speaking in front of so many felt daunting, but he remembered that he was among friends who had supported him. He stepped forward, his voice steady but humble.

"I learned that courage isn't just about facing what scares us," he began, his gaze sweeping over the crowd. "It's about trusting in ourselves and in those around us. My journey taught me to move with patience, to listen to the guidance of others, and to keep going, even when I felt uncertain."

The animals listened intently, their faces reflecting admiration and understanding. Linden felt a surge of confidence, realizing that his story could inspire others to find their own courage.

Ula, the wise owl, hooted softly, her eyes shining with approval. "Linden, your journey through the fog showed us the value of trusting in our inner voice," she said. "In moments of uncertainty, you reminded us that there is wisdom within each of us, waiting to guide us if we listen. Will you share with us how you learned to trust yourself?"

Linden nodded, remembering his journey through the foggy forest. "When I couldn't see the path, I had to rely on my other senses and my instincts," he said. "It was scary at first, but I learned that sometimes, we have to look within ourselves for guidance. Trusting our inner voice can lead us through even the darkest places."

A ripple of agreement spread through the crowd, and Linden felt a warm sense of connection with those around him. His experiences were not just his own; they were lessons that could help everyone in the jungle find strength and courage.

Balthazar the bear stepped forward, his gentle voice carrying a deep resonance. "Your journey showed us the strength of kindness, Linden," he said, his gaze filled with warmth. "You acted with compassion, even in moments of fear, and in doing so, you brought us all closer. Tell us, young lion, what kindness has taught you about courage."

Linden thought for a moment, choosing his words carefully. "I realized that kindness isn't just about helping others; it's about seeing the value in every creature, every experience," he said. "Each friend I met taught me something valuable, and together, we became stronger. Kindness is a part of courage, because it connects us and reminds us that we're never truly alone."

The crowd murmured in agreement, and Linden felt the warmth of their understanding. The jungle, once a vast and sometimes intimidating place, now felt like a close-knit family, bound together by shared experiences and values.

As the animals took turns speaking, sharing their own stories of courage and kindness, Linden realized that the council had become a gathering of shared wisdom, each creature adding their voice to the collective understanding of what it meant to be brave. Every story told, every lesson shared, added a new layer to the jungle's strength, reinforcing the bonds between them.

THE COURAGEOUS QUEST OF LITTLE LEO

After the council, Grizelda announced a time of celebration. Animals spread out in groups, sharing food, stories, and laughter. Linden found himself surrounded by friends, each one eager to thank him and share in the joy of the day.

Penny was by his side, her eyes sparkling with pride. "Linden, you brought the jungle together in a way that few could," she said, her voice filled with warmth. "Your courage and kindness have become a part of us all."

Linden smiled, feeling a deep sense of fulfillment. "I couldn't have done it alone," he replied. "Each friend, each lesson, became a part of my courage. The jungle feels like home because of all of you."

As the sun began to set, casting a golden glow over the gathering, Linden felt a sense of peace. The jungle had become a place of unity, filled with creatures who understood that courage was more than facing challenges; it was about building connections, acting with kindness, and supporting each other through life's ups and downs.

The Great Jungle Council had marked a new beginning, a time of unity and shared strength that would carry them all forward. And as Linden looked around at the faces of his friends, he knew that he was part of something truly special—a family bound by love, courage, and an unbreakable bond.

Chapter 20: The Unexpected Visitor

Days passed after the Great Jungle Council, and a sense of peace and harmony settled over the jungle. Linden continued his daily routines, visiting friends and sharing stories, feeling more connected to the jungle and its creatures than ever before. The courage he had gained from his journey filled him with a quiet confidence, and he found joy in each new day, knowing that his actions had brought happiness and unity to the jungle.

One morning, as the sun rose, casting golden light over the trees, Linden was relaxing by Penny's tree, watching the first birds take flight. Penny was nearby, her feathers shimmering in the sunlight as she hummed a soft tune, filling the air with warmth and comfort. Linden felt a deep sense of peace, grateful for the friendship they shared and the journey they had undertaken together.

Suddenly, the sound of hurried footsteps caught his attention. A small, panicked figure appeared on the path—a squirrel with bright, alert eyes and a bushy tail that twitched with nervous energy. He glanced around, his gaze finally landing on Linden and Penny.

"Linden! Penny!" the squirrel called, his voice filled with urgency. "You have to come quickly!"

Linden's heart skipped a beat as he stood, concern flashing in his eyes. "What's wrong?" he asked, his voice calm but attentive.

"It's... it's a stranger!" the squirrel replied, his voice barely a whisper. "A large creature, unlike anything we've ever seen, has entered the jungle. He's moving slowly, and he seems lost, but some of the animals are worried. No one knows where he's from or what he wants."

Linden exchanged a glance with Penny, sensing the worry that lingered in the air. "A stranger?" Penny murmured, tilting her head thoughtfully. "Perhaps he's just looking for help."

Linden nodded, a calm determination settling over him. "Let's go see if he needs assistance," he said, his voice steady. "No one should feel unwelcome in our jungle."

Together with the squirrel, Linden and Penny followed the winding path through the trees until they reached a small clearing near the edge of the jungle. There, surrounded by a cautious crowd of animals, stood a creature unlike any Linden had ever seen. He was large, with thick, shaggy fur and wide, gentle eyes that held a look of confusion. His long trunk moved slowly, feeling the ground as if searching for something.

Linden recognized him immediately from stories he had heard—this creature was an elephant. Though elephants were not native to this part of the jungle, Linden remembered stories of their intelligence, strength, and gentle nature. He noticed the way the elephant moved carefully, as though mindful of his surroundings, and his expression held no threat, only uncertainty.

Linden approached cautiously, stopping at a respectful distance. "Hello," he called gently, his voice calm and welcoming. "My name is Linden. You're in our jungle. Are you lost?"

The elephant turned, his eyes settling on Linden with a look of relief and gratitude. "Hello, Linden," he said in a deep, rumbling voice. "My name is Bala. I am indeed lost. I have traveled far from my home, and I seem to have wandered into unfamiliar territory. I didn't mean to startle anyone."

Linden offered a reassuring smile. "You're welcome here, Bala," he replied. "Our jungle has a place for everyone, and we would be glad to help you find your way."

Bala looked around, his expression filled with appreciation and relief. "Thank you, Linden," he said, his voice filled with warmth. "I was separated from my herd during a storm and have been wandering for days, unsure of where to go. I miss my family, but I am grateful to have found such kindness here."

Penny stepped forward, her voice gentle and understanding. "Bala, you don't have to worry. We can help you find a place to rest and gather whatever you need for your journey."

As the animals around them began to relax, Linden noticed that their initial fear had softened into curiosity. They watched Bala with interest, some even approaching to offer him food or water. Linden felt a sense of pride, knowing that his own journey of courage and kindness had inspired others to welcome this stranger with open hearts.

Grizelda, the wise gorilla, approached Bala, her gaze filled with respect. "Bala, your strength and resilience are evident," she said warmly. "Any creature who braves the unknown in search of family is a friend of ours. While you are here, you are one of us."

Kyro, the crocodile, gave a slow nod of approval. "Our jungle may be small compared to your homeland, but we will do what we can to support you," he said, his voice steady. "Feel free to rest here until you are ready to continue your journey."

Bala's eyes filled with gratitude as he looked at the animals around him. "Thank you, all of you," he said, his voice thick with emotion. "Your kindness reminds me of home, and it eases the sorrow of being separated from my family."

Linden sensed Bala's sadness, the way his heart ached for his herd. He approached the elephant, a gentle smile on his face. "Bala, would you like to share stories of your homeland with us?" he asked. "Sometimes, sharing memories can make the distance feel a little smaller."

Bala's face brightened, and he nodded gratefully. "I would be honored, Linden," he replied. "In my homeland, the savannas stretch as far as the eye can see, and the sunsets are a fiery orange that sets the sky ablaze. My herd and I would travel together, sharing stories and songs under the stars."

As Bala spoke, the animals gathered around, listening intently. His voice carried a richness that painted vivid pictures of his homeland, and

Linden could almost see the vast plains, feel the warmth of the savanna sun, and hear the calls of other elephants echoing in the distance. Bala's memories brought a sense of awe and wonder to the jungle, connecting everyone to a world beyond their own.

When Bala finished speaking, there was a moment of silence as the animals absorbed the beauty of his stories. Penny spoke up, her voice filled with admiration. "Your homeland sounds magnificent, Bala. Thank you for sharing it with us."

Bala shook his head, his gaze soft. "And thank you for listening," he replied. "Though I am far from home, your kindness has made me feel welcome. I may be lost, but I have found friends."

The animals cheered softly, their faces reflecting the warmth of Bala's words. Linden felt a surge of pride and gratitude, knowing that his jungle was a place where even strangers could feel at home. He approached Bala once more, his voice gentle.

Chapter 21: The Storm's Trial

Days after welcoming Bala, the jungle seemed alive with new stories, laughter, and shared memories. Bala had become a cherished guest, spending his days sharing tales of the savanna and teaching the jungle animals about the customs of his homeland. His kindness and gentle nature brought joy to everyone around him, and Linden felt proud to have helped create a space where new friendships could flourish.

One afternoon, as Linden and Penny sat by the river with a group of friends, Kyro the crocodile lifted his snout to the air, sniffing thoughtfully. His sharp eyes narrowed as he looked toward the sky, which had turned a shade darker than usual, the edges of the clouds tinged with a hint of gray.

"Something's coming," Kyro said in a low voice, his tone cautious. "I can feel it in the air."

Linden looked up, noticing the sudden chill in the breeze. The sky above was changing quickly, the clouds gathering and thickening into a dark, swirling mass. A sense of unease settled over the jungle, and animals began to murmur in worried voices, glancing around as though expecting the unexpected.

"What's happening?" Penny asked, her voice tinged with concern.

Balthazar the bear, who had joined them at the river, stood tall, his gaze fixed on the sky. "It's a storm," he said, his voice calm but serious. "And by the look of it, a powerful one. We should prepare."

The jungle had experienced storms before, but something about this one felt different, more intense. Linden felt a shiver of apprehension, but he took a deep breath, reminding himself of the courage and resilience he had developed over his journey. He knew that his role was to help keep everyone calm and to act as a leader in these moments of uncertainty.

Turning to Penny, Kyro, and Balthazar, Linden spoke with a steady voice. "Let's make sure everyone is safe," he said. "We need to help each other find shelter and keep calm."

The animals around him nodded, their fear easing as they looked to Linden for guidance. Together, they began to spread out across the jungle, calling to the animals and directing them toward safer areas. Linden and Penny worked side by side, leading smaller creatures to dens, hollow trees, and sheltered clearings where they could weather the storm together.

As the wind began to pick up, Bala the elephant helped by creating makeshift shelters with fallen branches and leaves, using his strength to provide protection for the animals that needed it. His calm, steady presence was reassuring, and he worked tirelessly, his focus on the safety of those around him.

Kyro guided animals near the river to higher ground, his sharp instincts alert to the potential danger of rising water levels. Balthazar used his strength to move larger branches and create a barrier around a central clearing, giving the animals a safe place to gather. Ula the owl flew from tree to tree, calling to those who were lost or frightened and guiding them to the sheltered areas.

The storm descended quickly, bringing with it a fierce wind that howled through the trees, bending branches and sending leaves swirling through the air. Thunder rumbled in the distance, and flashes of lightning lit up the darkening sky. Despite the chaos, Linden remained focused, his courage unwavering as he continued to help animals find safety.

As the rain began to pour, Linden huddled with a group of smaller animals beneath a large, sturdy tree, its branches providing a natural shelter. He spoke soothingly to them, telling stories of bravery and resilience, his calm voice a source of comfort amidst the storm. Penny perched nearby, her soft melodies rising above the sound of the rain, bringing peace to those around her.

Hours passed as the storm raged on, testing the patience and courage of every creature in the jungle. But despite the intensity of the storm, the animals remained calm, each one drawing strength from the unity they shared. Linden felt a deep sense of pride as he watched his friends, each one showing bravery in their own way, supporting one another with kindness and compassion.

As the storm began to subside, a sense of relief spread through the jungle. The rain slowed to a gentle drizzle, and the wind softened, leaving only the sound of water dripping from the leaves. Slowly, the animals emerged from their shelters, their faces filled with gratitude and joy. Despite the damage caused by the storm, everyone was safe, thanks to the courage and teamwork they had shown.

Linden stood with Penny, Bala, Kyro, and Balthazar, looking around at the jungle, which now glistened under the soft light of the setting sun. Though trees had fallen and branches littered the ground, the animals were unharmed, their spirits lifted by the strength they had found in each other.

Bala approached Linden, a gentle smile on his face. "Linden, your leadership helped us all stay calm and find safety," he said warmly. "You have brought this jungle together in ways I have never seen before."

Linden felt a flush of humility at Bala's words, his heart swelling with gratitude. "I couldn't have done it alone," he replied. "Everyone here showed courage and kindness. We supported each other, and that's what kept us safe."

Kyro gave a slow nod of approval, his eyes reflecting respect. "You may be young, Linden," he said, "but you have the heart of a true leader. This storm reminded us of the importance of unity, and you were the one who brought us together."

The animals around them murmured in agreement, their eyes filled with admiration. Linden realized that his journey had come full circle—not only had he learned courage and resilience, but he had also inspired others to find the same strength within themselves. The jungle was a place of harmony and friendship, a family bound together by shared values and unwavering support.

As the animals began to clean up and restore their homes, Linden worked alongside them, helping to clear fallen branches and rebuild shelters. Penny, Bala, Kyro, and Balthazar worked by his side, each one bringing their unique strengths to the task. Together, they restored the jungle to its former beauty, their hearts filled with gratitude for the safety they had found in one another.

That evening, as the stars appeared in the clear night sky, the animals gathered once more, this time to celebrate their resilience and the bonds that had kept them strong through the storm. They shared food, stories, and laughter, their spirits lifted by the knowledge that they could face any challenge together.

Penny began to sing, her voice a soft, joyful melody that filled the clearing. The animals joined in, their voices rising in harmony, a song of unity and gratitude that echoed through the jungle. Linden closed his eyes, letting the music fill his heart, knowing that he was a part of something truly special—a community built on courage, kindness, and friendship.

Chapter 22: A Gift from the Stars

The jungle recovered from the storm, a sense of peace and gratitude filling the air. Every creature had contributed to restoring their home, and the unity they had displayed during the storm created a deeper bond among them all. Linden felt more connected than ever to his friends, knowing that each one was a part of the strength that carried them through every challenge.

One evening, as twilight cast a gentle glow over the jungle, Linden and Penny decided to take a walk together, enjoying the calmness that followed the storm. The air was fresh, filled with the scent of rain-washed leaves and wildflowers, and the sky above was a deepening shade of blue, dotted with the first stars of the night.

As they walked along a quiet path, Penny looked up at the sky, her eyes reflecting the stars. "Look, Linden," she said softly, "isn't it beautiful? The stars seem brighter than ever tonight."

Linden nodded, gazing up at the vast sky with wonder. The stars twinkled like distant lanterns, filling the night with a sense of magic and mystery. "It's amazing," he replied, his voice filled with awe. "It feels like they're watching over us."

Penny smiled, her gaze thoughtful. "My grandmother used to tell me stories about the stars," she said. "She said they are like wise old friends, guiding us and reminding us that there's always light, even in the darkest times."

Linden listened, feeling a warmth spread through him at Penny's words. He loved the idea of the stars as old friends, silent guardians who offered their light and wisdom to those who sought it.

As they continued their walk, they came upon a small clearing, where the starlight shone down through the trees, illuminating a patch of ground covered in soft moss and wildflowers. The scene was enchanting, as though the stars had chosen this spot to share a special moment with the jungle.

THE COURAGEOUS QUEST OF LITTLE LEO

Linden and Penny sat down together, looking up at the sky, their hearts filled with peace. After a few quiet moments, Penny began to hum a gentle melody, her voice blending with the sounds of the night. Her song was soft and serene, carrying a feeling of calm that seemed to reach up toward the stars themselves.

As she sang, something remarkable happened. A single star, brighter than the rest, seemed to twinkle more intensely, as if responding to Penny's song. Linden watched in awe as the star's light grew stronger, casting a soft glow over the clearing. He felt a tingling sensation, a sense that something magical was about to unfold.

Then, slowly, the star's light began to descend, drifting down from the sky like a gentle mist. The glow filled the air, shimmering like silver dust, and enveloped Linden and Penny, bathing them in a soft, warm light. It was as though the stars were sending them a gift, a blessing of sorts, and Linden felt his heart swell with gratitude and wonder.

Penny stopped singing, her eyes wide with amazement. "Linden," she whispered, her voice filled with awe, "do you feel it?"

Linden nodded, barely able to speak. "Yes, Penny," he replied softly. "It feels like... like the stars are sharing their light with us."

The gentle glow surrounded them, and Linden felt a warmth in his chest, a sensation of peace and love that seemed to flow through him, filling every corner of his heart. He closed his eyes, allowing himself to be fully present in the moment, to embrace the gift of light and wonder that the stars had given them.

In that moment, memories of his journey flooded his mind—the challenges he had faced, the friends he had made, the courage he had discovered within himself. He realized that every step, every lesson, had led him to this place, to this moment of pure gratitude and joy. He understood that his journey had not only been one of courage but also one of connection, a journey that had deepened his bond with the world around him.

As the starlight slowly faded, leaving only a soft glow that lingered in their hearts, Linden opened his eyes, feeling a newfound sense of purpose. He looked at Penny, who was gazing at him with a look of deep understanding.

"Linden," she said softly, her voice filled with emotion, "I think the stars are telling us that we are never alone. No matter where our journeys take us, we are always connected to each other and to the world around us."

Linden nodded, feeling the truth of her words. He realized that his journey had given him more than courage; it had given him a sense of belonging, a knowledge that he was part of something greater, a community of friends, and a world filled with beauty and light.

The two of them sat in silence for a while, savoring the peace that filled the clearing. The stars continued to twinkle above, their light steady and reassuring, as if reminding Linden and Penny that they were indeed part of something timeless and wonderful.

After a while, Linden spoke, his voice soft but filled with conviction. "Penny, I want to share what I've learned with others," he said. "There are so many creatures who might be facing their own challenges, who might feel alone. I want to help them find their courage, to show them that they are never truly alone."

Penny's eyes sparkled with pride. "That's a wonderful idea, Linden," she replied. "Your journey has been filled with wisdom, and by sharing it, you can inspire others to find their own paths, just as you did."

Linden felt a surge of excitement at the thought. He knew that his journey was not just his own—it was a gift he could share with others, a way to help those who needed guidance, courage, or a reminder of the beauty in the world.

The stars continued to shine above, and as Linden looked up at them, he made a silent promise to himself and to the jungle. He would carry forward the light he had received, spreading kindness and courage wherever he went. His journey had taught him that courage was not just about facing fear; it was about choosing to make a difference, to bring hope and love to those around him.

As the night grew darker, Linden and Penny returned to their home, their hearts filled with peace and purpose. They knew that the journey would continue, that there would always be new challenges, new friends, and new lessons. But they were ready, knowing that they had each other and the strength of the jungle to guide them.

From that night on, Linden began sharing his stories with others, teaching the young animals about courage, kindness, and the wisdom of the jungle. He became a mentor to those who sought guidance, a friend to those who needed comfort, and a source of strength for those who faced uncertainty.

Chapter 23: The Teaching Tree

In the days following that magical night under the stars, Linden felt an unshakable purpose. He was determined to fulfill his promise to share the wisdom and courage he had gained with others in the jungle. Each morning, he would walk through the forest, meeting young animals and telling them stories from his journey. The lessons he shared filled his heart with joy, and the young animals listened with wide eyes, inspired by his tales.

One day, as Linden and Penny walked together, Penny had an idea. "Linden," she began thoughtfully, "you have a gift for sharing what you've learned. But have you ever thought about creating a special place where others could come to hear your stories and learn from you?"

Linden's eyes brightened with excitement. "That's a wonderful idea, Penny!" he exclaimed. "A place where anyone who seeks courage, wisdom, or comfort could come. A place where I could pass on what I've learned and inspire others."

Penny's face lit up with a smile. "We could make it somewhere special, a place in the heart of the jungle where everyone feels welcome. We could call it the Teaching Tree."

Linden loved the name, and together, they began searching for the perfect spot. They wandered through the jungle, exploring quiet groves and hidden clearings, looking for a place that felt just right. After a while, they came to a large, ancient tree nestled in a clearing surrounded by wildflowers. Its branches were wide and sturdy, providing shade and shelter, and its roots stretched deep into the earth, giving it a sense of wisdom and stability.

"This is it," Linden said, gazing up at the tree in awe. "This will be the Teaching Tree."

Penny nodded in agreement, her eyes filled with joy. "It's perfect," she said. "It's strong, welcoming, and full of life. Just like the lessons you'll teach here."

The two friends spent the next few days preparing the area around the Teaching Tree. They cleared away fallen branches, arranged soft moss and leaves for seating, and decorated the area with colorful flowers. The animals of the jungle, hearing of their plans, began to pitch in, each one bringing something to contribute. Squirrels gathered acorns and nuts for visitors, birds brought feathers and bright leaves for decoration, and even the insects added to the beauty of the area with their delicate patterns on the flowers.

Finally, the Teaching Tree was ready. Word spread quickly, and on the first day, animals from all over the jungle gathered to see what Linden had created. The atmosphere was filled with excitement, and Linden felt a rush of gratitude as he looked out at the gathering of eager faces, each one a reminder of the friendships he had formed and the journey that had brought him here.

Linden took a deep breath, then began to speak, his voice steady and warm. "Welcome, friends, to the Teaching Tree," he said, his gaze filled with kindness. "This place is for anyone who seeks wisdom, courage, or simply a reminder that they are not alone. Here, we'll share stories, learn from each other, and grow together."

The animals listened intently, their eyes shining with curiosity and admiration. Linden continued, telling them stories of his journey to find the singing tree, the challenges he had faced, and the friends who had helped him along the way. He spoke of Grizelda's lesson in patience, Kyro's teachings on respect, and Balthazar's wisdom about kindness.

After each story, he would invite the animals to share their own experiences, encouraging them to find the lessons within their own lives. One by one, they spoke up, their voices filled with pride and bravery as they shared tales of overcoming fears, helping friends, and discovering their own strengths.

One young rabbit, whose ears twitched nervously as she spoke, shared her story of overcoming her fear of the river. "At first, I was so scared to cross," she said softly. "But then I remembered Linden's story about respecting the flow of the water, and I tried to be patient. It took time, but I learned to trust myself and made it across."

The animals clapped and cheered for her, their support filling the air with warmth. Linden felt a deep pride in the young rabbit, knowing that his story had inspired her to find her own courage. He realized that the Teaching Tree was not just a place for him to share his journey but a place where everyone could grow together, learning from each other's experiences.

Penny, watching from a nearby branch, sang a soft, joyful melody, her song filling the clearing with a sense of harmony and peace. Her music reminded everyone of the beauty in their shared journey, and Linden felt a deep sense of fulfillment, knowing that his vision for the Teaching Tree was becoming a reality.

As the day continued, more animals stepped forward, each one sharing a lesson they had learned. A young fox spoke about learning patience while waiting for his food, a bird shared her story of finding courage to explore new heights, and even Kyro, the usually quiet crocodile, shared a story about learning respect for his fellow creatures.

With each story, Linden saw the jungle come alive with understanding and unity. He realized that every creature, no matter how small or shy, had wisdom to share, and he felt honored to be a part of their growth. The Teaching Tree had become a place of learning, compassion, and connection, a place where courage and kindness flourished.

At the end of the day, as the sun began to set, Linden gathered everyone around the tree for one final message. "Thank you, friends, for sharing your stories," he said, his voice filled with emotion. "The courage you have shown here today is the foundation of this place. The Teaching Tree is not just mine—it belongs to all of us. Every story you share, every lesson you teach, adds to the strength and beauty of our jungle."

The animals cheered, their voices blending together in a joyous harmony. Linden felt a profound sense of peace, knowing that the Teaching Tree would continue to grow, nourished by the wisdom and love of everyone who visited. This place, he realized, was more than just a gathering spot; it was a testament to the power of community and the courage that lived within each creature.

Chapter 24: The Journey of a New Friend

Word of the Teaching Tree spread throughout the jungle as animals from near and far came to listen to Linden's stories and share their own. The Teaching Tree had become a place of gathering, learning, and healing, where creatures of all ages came together, united by their desire for courage, wisdom, and friendship. Linden found joy in seeing others grow, and he knew that the jungle had become stronger through the bonds they had built.

One morning, as Linden prepared to open the Teaching Tree for a new day of stories, he noticed a small creature approaching the clearing. She was a young hedgehog, her spines soft and her eyes wide with a mixture of curiosity and timidity. She moved slowly, almost hesitantly, as if unsure of her place among the gathering animals.

Linden approached her with a warm smile, lowering his voice to a gentle tone. "Hello," he greeted kindly. "Welcome to the Teaching Tree. My name is Linden. What's yours?"

The little hedgehog looked up at him, her gaze cautious but intrigued. "I... I'm Hazel," she replied softly, her voice barely more than a whisper. "I heard about this place and... I thought maybe... maybe I could come and listen."

Linden's heart warmed, and he nodded encouragingly. "Of course, Hazel. The Teaching Tree is open to everyone. You're welcome here."

Hazel's eyes softened with relief, and she gave a small nod before settling down at the edge of the clearing. Linden could sense her shyness, but he was glad that she had found the courage to come. As more animals arrived, he began his usual storytelling, sharing lessons about courage, kindness, and the strength found in friendship. Each story was met with cheers, smiles, and thoughtful nods, and Linden felt fulfilled as he watched his friends absorb the wisdom of his journey.

Throughout the morning, he noticed Hazel listening intently, her small face filled with wonder as she took in each story. When he

THE COURAGEOUS QUEST OF LITTLE LEO 97

finished speaking, Linden encouraged the animals to share their own experiences, and one by one, they stepped forward, each story adding to the warmth and unity of the group.

Finally, Linden turned to Hazel, his voice gentle. "Hazel, would you like to share something with us?" he asked, hoping to make her feel included.

Hazel looked around, her eyes widening with a mixture of surprise and nervousness. She hesitated, glancing down at her paws, and for a moment Linden thought she might not feel ready. But then, with a deep breath, Hazel lifted her head, her voice trembling but determined.

"I... I've always been afraid of making new friends," she began, her gaze fixed on the ground. "I'm so small and... and different from everyone else. Sometimes, I feel like I don't belong."

Linden listened closely, his heart filling with empathy. He understood the courage it took for Hazel to speak up, to voice her fears in front of the group. Around them, the other animals watched her with kindness and understanding, each one sensing her vulnerability and respecting her bravery.

Hazel continued, her voice growing stronger. "But when I heard about the Teaching Tree... I thought maybe it would be different. I thought maybe I could find a place where I could feel... safe."

Penny, who had been listening from a nearby branch, chimed in with a warm smile. "Hazel, you're always welcome here," she said softly. "The Teaching Tree is for everyone, and we're glad you're here with us."

Encouraged by the support, Hazel's face lit up with a shy smile. "Thank you," she said, her voice filled with gratitude. "I've always wanted to be brave, like the animals in Linden's stories. I thought that maybe, by coming here, I could learn to be like that too."

Linden moved closer to Hazel, his expression filled with warmth. "Hazel," he said gently, "you're already brave. It takes courage to come to a new place and share your heart with others. The strength you've shown by being here today is exactly the kind of bravery that makes this jungle special."

The other animals nodded in agreement, their expressions filled with admiration for Hazel. Linden could see her shoulders relax, her small frame settling into a more comfortable stance as she absorbed the support around her. He knew that moments like these were the reason he had created the Teaching Tree—a place where every creature, no matter their size or background, could find courage and belonging.

Throughout the day, Hazel stayed close, listening to stories and learning from the wisdom of others. As the animals continued to share, she found herself growing more comfortable, her initial shyness giving way to a sense of connection. Linden noticed the change in her, and he felt a sense of pride in her growth.

Later, as the sun dipped lower in the sky, casting a warm, golden light over the clearing, Linden called for everyone's attention. "Before we finish for the day, I'd like to share something important," he said, his voice calm but full of purpose. "Each of you has shown incredible courage by being here, by sharing your stories and supporting one another. This place is not just mine; it belongs to all of us. The courage we find here grows stronger because we share it."

The animals around him nodded, their eyes shining with understanding. Linden's words resonated deeply, and he felt a warmth in his heart, knowing that the Teaching Tree had become a beacon of hope and strength for everyone.

Turning to Hazel, Linden offered her a warm smile. "Hazel, would you join me up here?" he asked gently.

Hazel looked surprised, but she nodded, her small feet carrying her to his side. Linden placed a gentle paw on her shoulder, his gaze filled with pride.

"Hazel has shown us that bravery comes in many forms," he said, his voice steady and kind. "By facing her fears, she has reminded us all of the strength it takes to be vulnerable and open. Hazel, you are a part of this place, and we are grateful to have you with us."

The animals erupted into applause, their voices filled with warmth and acceptance. Hazel's face lit up with joy, her eyes sparkling with gratitude. She looked around at her new friends, her heart full of a sense of belonging that she had never felt before.

Chapter 25: The Legacy of Courage

The Teaching Tree had become a cornerstone of life in the jungle, a place where creatures of all ages came to learn, share, and grow together. Every day, new faces joined familiar ones, and Linden's stories became woven into the fabric of the community, inspiring courage, kindness, and unity. With each gathering, Linden felt the strength of the jungle grow, a shared strength that radiated outwards like sunlight, warming every heart it touched.

One afternoon, as Linden prepared for another day at the Teaching Tree, he noticed a group of young animals huddled together, whispering excitedly. At their center was Hazel, her small face bright with enthusiasm as she shared something with her friends. Linden watched with a smile, feeling a deep sense of pride as he realized how much she had grown.

As he approached, Hazel and her friends looked up, their eyes lighting up with excitement. "Linden!" Hazel called, her voice strong and confident. "We've been talking, and… well, we want to do something special for the Teaching Tree. Something to show how much it means to all of us."

Linden's heart warmed, and he nodded, encouraging her to continue. "What do you have in mind, Hazel?"

Hazel glanced at her friends, then back at Linden, her eyes shining with pride. "We want to create a place nearby where we can plant seeds. A garden! It can be a gift for the Teaching Tree, and each of us can plant something to show our gratitude and to keep the spirit of courage growing."

Linden's heart swelled with admiration. "That's a beautiful idea, Hazel," he said warmly. "A garden of courage, where everyone can leave something that represents their journey. I think the Teaching Tree would be honored."

The young animals cheered, their faces glowing with excitement as they imagined the new garden. Hazel beamed with pride, and Linden felt a deep gratitude for the love and unity that had blossomed around the Teaching Tree. He knew that the garden would become a living testament to the strength and kindness that bound them together.

Over the next few days, animals from all over the jungle joined in to help create the garden. Some brought seeds, others gathered soil and water, and each one left a small mark of their gratitude. Birds flew overhead, sprinkling feathers and petals, while squirrels and rabbits helped dig small holes for planting. Even Bala, the elephant who had once been a stranger, used his strength to carry water and ensure that each new plant had the nourishment it needed to grow.

As the garden began to take shape, Linden looked around, his heart swelling with pride. Every plant, every flower, every tiny seed was a symbol of courage, a reminder of the journeys that each animal had taken to reach this place of unity and peace.

On the day the garden was completed, Linden invited everyone to gather around the Teaching Tree for a special ceremony. As the sun cast a warm golden light over the clearing, the animals assembled, their faces filled with joy and pride as they looked upon the garden they had created together.

Linden stood before them, his heart brimming with gratitude. "Friends," he began, his voice carrying the warmth of his love for each of them, "today we celebrate not just the Teaching Tree, but the courage and kindness that each of you has shown. This garden is a gift from all of us, a reminder that our strength grows from the roots of unity, compassion, and courage."

The animals listened, their eyes shining with understanding. Linden continued, his gaze sweeping over the garden. "Each plant here represents a journey, a story of courage that has brought us all closer. The Teaching Tree and this garden are symbols of the love and strength that we share. They are reminders that no matter where we go or what challenges we face, we are never truly alone."

A murmur of agreement spread through the crowd, and Linden felt a deep peace settle over him. He knew that the garden would grow alongside the Teaching Tree, a testament to the courage that bound the jungle together.

Hazel stepped forward, a small flower held delicately in her paws. "Linden," she said, her voice filled with emotion, "on behalf of all of us, thank you for sharing your journey with us. Thank you for showing us that courage is something we all have inside."

Linden felt a lump form in his throat as he looked at Hazel, his heart overflowing with gratitude. "Thank you, Hazel," he replied softly. "Your courage has inspired me, and it's shown me that the strength of this jungle lies in each of you. Together, we create a legacy that will live on in every heart, every leaf, and every star above."

One by one, the animals came forward to plant their own tokens in the garden, each one adding a unique touch to the vibrant tapestry of flowers, herbs, and tiny plants. Some left small stones, others placed feathers or leaves, each gift a personal symbol of gratitude, courage, and love.

As the ceremony drew to a close, Linden looked out over the garden, feeling a profound sense of fulfillment. He knew that the Teaching Tree and the garden would continue to inspire future generations, reminding them of the strength that came from unity and the courage that grew from kindness.

That evening, as the stars appeared in the sky, Linden sat beneath the Teaching Tree, his gaze fixed on the garden that now blossomed nearby. Penny sat beside him, her song filling the night with a melody that seemed to echo the love and peace that filled the jungle.

"Linden," Penny said softly, her voice filled with warmth, "you've created something truly beautiful here. The Teaching Tree and the garden are not just places—they're a legacy, a reminder of everything you've shared with us."

Linden nodded, his heart filled with gratitude. "I couldn't have done it alone, Penny," he replied. "Every friend, every lesson, every act of courage and kindness brought us to this moment. This is not just my story—it's the story of everyone who found courage here."

Penny smiled, her eyes reflecting the gentle starlight. "And because of you, that story will continue to grow, inspiring others to find their own courage."

As they sat together beneath the stars, Linden felt a deep peace, knowing that his journey had come full circle. He had discovered courage, not just for himself but for the entire jungle. He had learned that true strength lay in the connections he shared, the kindness he gave, and the unity that bound them all together.

In the heart of the jungle, surrounded by friends and the legacy of courage they had built, Linden knew that he was exactly where he was meant to be. The journey would continue, filled with new stories, new challenges, and new faces. And with each new day, the Teaching Tree and the garden would remind every creature of the love and strength that brought them together.

Don't miss out!

Visit the website below and you can sign up to receive emails whenever Callum West publishes a new book. There's no charge and no obligation.

https://books2read.com/r/B-A-WMHVC-OFMIF

BOOKS 2 READ

Connecting independent readers to independent writers.

About the Publisher

Kids Publishing is a vibrant and innovative publishing company dedicated to creating captivating, educational, and inspiring children's books. Specializing in diverse genres, from enchanting bedtime stories to engaging tales of diversity, inclusion, and moral values, Kids Publishing aims to ignite imagination and foster positive character development in young readers aged 3 to 12. With a team of talented authors, illustrators, and editors, the company delivers high-quality books that combine creativity with life lessons. Committed to shaping future generations, Kids Publishing ensures every story nurtures curiosity, empathy, and a love for reading, empowering children to dream big and embrace their unique potential.

Milton Keynes UK
Ingram Content Group UK Ltd.
UKHW020914291124
451807UK00013B/916